SPILLWAY

Stories by
KIM BRADLEY

STEPHEN F. AUSTIN STATE UNIVERSITY PRESS

For more information:
Stephen F. Austin State University Press
P.O. Box 13007 SFA Station
Nacogdoches, Texas 75962
sfapress@sfasu.edu
www.sfasu.edu/sfapress

Managing Editor: Kimberly Verhines
Book Design: Meredith Janning
Cover Design: Meredith Janning
Cover Art: Marseas via Getty Images
Distributed by Texas A&M Consortium
www.tamupress.com

ISBN: 978-1-62288-235-9

In memory of my favorite storyteller,
my dad, Bob Bradley
1943-2014

Contents:

Cheating Time

JACKIE WANTED TO MAKE IT THE HONEST WAY, but her sister Cassie's letter was frantic: There was a lien on the house. She was driving a stolen truck. The power bill was overdue. Jackie's first night out of New Mexico Women's Correctional was not what she'd expected. Staring into the parched Espanola night from the cab of an 18-wheeler, the sage and brandy smell of a man named Ignacio on her skin—a man she'd never see again—Jackie realized there was nowhere to go but home to Hawthorne, Florida.

Folded inside her socks was the prison's farewell gift—ten crisp twenties that clung to her damp ankles, a furrowed fifty she'd taken from sleeping Ignacio's wallet. Behind her, the Greyhound's air brakes moaned; the bus moved down the muddy St. Johns River for Interlachen, Palatka, Hastings, St. Augustine. Two years had passed since she'd seen her sister, the limestone roads and pricked pines. From across the street, Cassie came running. "Jackie, I missed you so much, I went out and bought myself a bottle of Heaven Scent."

It took a minute, Jackie's chin resting on her sister's shoulder, before she recalled the blue-tinted perfume—bergamot, apple blossom, baby powder. She examined her sister's tired denim dress.

"You been wearing my clothes, too?"

Cassie kissed her cheek. "Now that wouldn't be respectful, would it?" She locked her arm around Jackie's slim waist and led her down Johnson Street.

"You make it sound like I've been dead." Though death, Jackie thought, was a good way to explain her years away. Now she was paroled. Reborn. At the empty lot on the corner, Old Man Caden's son tended a fire of water oak limbs and amber sweetgum leaves. He looked up at the sisters, stared Jackie right in the eye, then went back to work, rake tines grating the sidewalk's crumbling concrete.

"He doesn't even remember me," Jackie said.

Ahead on the corner was their house, thick potato vines braiding the porch railings, their spent roots dropping down like testicles, the once-white house paint peeling in ragged scrolls. The tannic ditch water smelled of red wine.

"I'm tired," Jackie said, wondering if Cassie had taken her sweaters, too. She wasn't used to the humidity that gave the December air a bone chill and made frizzy red ringlets of her hair. "I'd love to put a fire in the fireplace tonight."

"You smell like Lysol, kid," Cassie said. "Get a hot shower while we still have water."

Cassie had set up the artificial Scotch pine like Jackie requested, but there were no ornaments, only snarled lights knotting the green torso. Jackie knelt at a cardboard box marked "CHRISTMAS." As a kid, she'd marched felt-legged elves across the mantle. She remembered a cotton-ball Santa, and a Popsicle-stick Star of Bethlehem buried in yellow glitter.

"No time to waste." Cassie snapped her fingers. "You read my letters. We need to catch folks while they got spending on their minds."

Jackie shoved the ornament box under the tree, and took a sweatshirt hanging from the door hook. She looked for gloves, settled on an orange knit hunting cap.

Cassie was a professional scammer. Once their father joked that Cassie was born with such a sweet talk that a man would believe she could siphon humidity from the Florida air. Cassie was successful because it came naturally to her, and she always stuck with a plan which was to make deals far from home, offer quick false fixes for a few bucks, then move on.

For years, she'd made her best cash during hurricane season.

Before the storms began June 1, she measured for protective shutters that were never created or delivered. When the season ended in November, she accessed damage, ran roofing scams and water quality scares promising fancy water filters. In 2007, all the good storms stopped, and Cassie changed gears. The letters she sent Jackie in the New Mexico prison had lists of invasive non-native plants and animals that could never be fully eradicated: Asian swamp eel, hydrilla, Japanese climbing fern, water hyacinth, Brazilian pepper plants, Monk Parakeets, Wild Hogs, European starlings. The way Cassie told it to Jackie, there were always new ways for cheating. And, delivered sincerely, any dishonest sales person could wrangle a few bucks from a good story.

Cassie diagnosed problems, whether homeowners had them or not, and if they didn't, she saw to it they acquired one. She set up a greenhouse out back of the house, and nurtured exotic seedlings that had only one goal in life and that was to root deep and kill out native species.

Jackie had always stayed out of Cassie's business. She'd found her hard luck the usual way—with a man she thought she'd loved. In prison, Jackie couldn't think about the big money Cassie's scams might bring. She had no use for dreams. She became obsessed with words Cassie had written on the pages. From behind bars, the lists of plants and animals read like poems.

"What did you decide?" Jackie asked.

"Trust me," Cassie said. She was the business woman, said the tone in her voice. She clasped Jackie's hand, inspected her fingers. "Let's talk about *your* letters. All fancy with typing. Show off, you."

Jackie and her cellmate Quinta Levoy took secretary courses at the prison, and Jackie caught on to typing. Quinta was dreadful, but a good sport. "Go, little mama, go," Quinta would say to Jackie. "There's fire in your fingers." Jackie blew through quick brown foxes jumping over fences. She imagined black letters searing crisp white paper.

Once, Quinta suggested Jackie take up piano on the outside, as if typed words on another instrument could become music. Jackie imagined a jazz of minor notes, cars shifting gears, acorns popping tin rooftops. In the black of her prison cell, Jackie declared that one day she'd make her living with typing. A good reliable boring job. Recording important notes. She yearned for the predictable to ground her. This was how they spoke at night when Quinta combed out her hair and said prayers.

"About your cozy fire," Cassie said, pointing to the plywood panel blocking the chimney opening. "Coons. Had one in here last night with his nose inside the Fruit Loops. Welcome home, Sis."

CASSIE LET HER DRIVE. Jackie figured the generosity stemmed from what could happen if they got caught in the stolen Chevrolet Custom Deluxe. The mustard paint was an attention-grabber, and the cranky beast was slow. "Somebody's bound to recognize this thing," Jackie said, grinding the gears into third.

"You always were the worry wart."

Driving, once Jackie became reacquainted with it, helped her think. Cassie mentioned she'd switched tags from a junk yard car. "That'll buy time."

"How much time do we need?" Jackie asked. She understood time more than anyone. She'd learned to tally hours, weeks, years. But all Cassie said was, "Enough," and when she grinned, her taut lips made Jackie's hands sweat.

THIS WAS NORTH CENTRAL FLORIDA'S lake country. The two-lane road cradled wide lakes, one after the next. Sparkling surfaces glared and winked at them from between cypress trees and shoreline bulrush. There were pairs of identical lakes, at least six called Twin Lakes; misshapen kidney lakes named for old men settlers – large and small versions of themselves—Big Fillmore, Little Fillmore, Big Macintyre, Little Macintyre.

A month ago, Cassie drove out here to Interlachen in the dark with mayonnaise jars of white flies she'd babied in a makeshift green house. She plundered yards and unleashed the pests on heirloom fuchsia azaleas; hibiscus bushes the size of cedar trees, golden mums in verdigris urns, Boston ferns fluming from hanging peat baskets.

Then, she'd made the first official visit informing folks of a white fly epidemic. "This may well be the worst of its kind in decades. We'll monitor it," she told the homeowners. "If the flies don't go away, I'll offer you my father's secret formula. At a bargain."

So this trip with Jackie was actually Cassie's third time back. At a red-brick rancher with three or more acres separating it from the next house, a kind-faced widow wearing gardening gloves and khaki pants met them in the drive. She was fit to be tied. White flies suffocated her garden with hideous powdery webs. She pointed to a pot of shriveled, shrouded yellow and purple pansies.

"Here I am," Cassie said. "A woman of my word. I said I'd check back if they weren't better." She acted as if she didn't care a hoot about money, that the health of these variegated annuals were all that mattered in the world.

"My revolutionary spray," Cassie held up an old Formula 409 bottle, the label scraped off. She doused the giant yellow-veined leaves of a Pothos vine that plaited the porch beams.

"Not only are they not better," Cassie said. "The white flies have spread." She pointed to the low-slug palms that rose no taller than her hips. They resembled marching green snails. She nudged Jackie.

"Your poor Sago's," Jackie said, taking the cue. She avoided eye contact with the old woman for fear she'd read deceit off her like a book.

Cassie bent, inspecting the pert, healthy fronds. "They are no doubt the carriers. We can't salvage them. I'm so sorry."

The woman put a gloved finger to her lips. "My," she said. "They look just fine to me."

"We'll dig them up," Cassie said, "Otherwise; the flies will tunnel and kill your azaleas, then your grass. At least now the webbing's contained on the exterior leaves."

Jackie shoveled; Cassie sprayed diluted Heaven Scent and cayenne pepper on the leaves. Jackie sneezed. She wondered where Cassie had heard words like *revolutionary, exterior, salvage.*

The woman squinted. "Dear, dear," she said. She was so appreciative the guilt made Jackie want to run, but Cassie clutched her elbow. Jackie stared at the ground.

"Well, of course," the woman said. "Please. Take them off my hands. I'll pay you good."

Back in the truck, Cassie counted the money.

"You get a kick out of doing people in, don't you?" Jackie said.

"Hell yeah, I do."

"Well, I don't," Jackie said. She had a headache. In the confines of the old truck, the perfume smelled of ripe pears and moth balls. She rolled down the window. How in the world had she worn Heaven Scent all those years?

"Slow down," Cassie said. "Watch the speed limit," but Jackie felt she was driving in slow motion. At a sign marked "Gainesville 12 Miles," Cassie directed her to a gravel one-lane road.

Cassie rubbed Jackie's neck. "I make it look easy, don't I, sis?"

Jackie thought about how Cassie roped people in with sweet talk so fast they didn't know what hit them. "You sure are a pro. I can't lie."

"Sis, it comes with practice."

From the way the oak leaves along the road were dusted with ghostly limestone sand, Jackie assumed it hadn't rained for months, but the air was sated with moisture. "Nobody ever called you on something?" Jackie asked.

Cassie counted the cash again. She put it inside an envelope, hid it under her seat. "They're not all gullible. I learned to tell which ones look like they could catch a girl in a lie and which ones couldn't."

"You make it sound like you can see it in their eyes."

"It's because I can, sister. I sure can." Cassie sounded so serious, so confident Jackie figured that was how she never got caught – she simply believed she couldn't be.

The road was narrow here. A lake's glaring surface squinted and accused them through a congested stand of camphor trees. "Turn," Cassie directed. The tires crackled over bristling fallen tree limbs and acorns. "We're almost here."

"Where is *here*?" Jackie asked. She dodged pot holes and a stray dog. Shovels and buckets rattled from the truck bed. The chassis trembled beneath them. Sweat beaded on Jackie's forehead. "The power steering's shot. You'd think somebody be grateful you took this off their hands."

"Keep driving," Cassie said. "It's up ahead."

Jackie needed to know exactly where they were, but she stayed quiet. Cassie wouldn't understand. Instead, Jackie tried to remember the cell she shared with Quinta, how over time the coarse green frayed sheets eventually felt soft against her face. How the setting sun through the tiny window turned Quinta's black hair bronze. That was the hardest part of freedom—leaving the comfort of knowing what would happen day in and day out. Here on the outside there was no predicting the next hour. Right now, at this moment in December 2008, Jackie didn't know where she was. Sleep would come hard without Quinta's melodic sleep talking. *Mis hijos, mis florecitos.* Jackie would even miss Quinta's haunted *pendejo* cries at the man who'd put her there. Suddenly, Jackie regretted never knowing what Quinta had been dreaming about all those nights.

"I wish I spoke Spanish," she said.

"Like hell you do," Cassie said. "Now look, you've gone and missed our turn."

AT THE END OF THE LONG LIMESTONE one-lane road, Cassie pointed toward a lake with shallow weedy banks, concrete block houses, and clapboard cabins on stilts with long spindly piers.

"Little Maul," she said.

Cassie nodded up the path at a man leaning on a walker, the kind Jackie remembered their father used in his last years, his palms gripping the rails in a death clinch. This man was weak and thin and grateful to see them. Cassie pulled on a sweater and white galoshes. At the shore, she knelt and reached with her left hand up to her elbows. She extracted a dribbling purple plant, its roots still clawing the sandy bottom.

"Beautiful," Jackie said.

The old man pounded the sand with the walker. "This shit? Beautiful?"

Cassie looked embarrassed. She pinched Jackie's elbow hard and whispered, "Keep your mouth shut, will you?"

Cassie turned sweetly to the old man. He'd hobbled closer. "My sister, Mr. Cecil, doesn't know what she's talking about. This is water hyacinth," Cassie said, talking to Jackie like she was a first grader. "Grows so fast it just about doubles every 12 days."

"Look over there," he pointed. Six-foot wide mats drifted toward them, then blew back with the breeze.

"New recruits," Cassie said.

"Goddamn things block the sunlight. Crowds out all the other good plants," Mr. Cecil said.

Then, Cassie turned to Jackie, and the tone in her voice was irritating as hell. She spoke like she was some smart scientist. "Water hyacinth uses up most of the available oxygen in water, killing the fish." She looked up to the old man, "But don't you worry about it, Mr. Cecil. We're here. Stand back now; watch that leg of yours."

"How *do* you get rid of it?" Jackie asked. They were at the truck bed, out of earshot. Cassie let down the tailgate, and seized a kettle of kerosene.

"We're going to set it on fire?" Jackie asked.

"You can't ever get rid of it, sis, but we'll say we can. I been farming these plants for months, and that old man is paying me to get rid of my own handiwork. Don't spoil this." Cassie looked up the bank. Mr. Cecil was anchored there on the shore by the hunched-railed walker. Jackie saw something in Cassie's expression that contained both evil and weariness. Jackie wondered how long her sister could work this business of cheating.

With white boots up to her knees, Cassie looked like a go-go dancer wading in the lake. She drizzled kerosene on the purple blooms. It seemed such a shame to Jackie. The flowers looked so dainty and harmless.

"How long will it take?" Mr. Cecil called. He'd abandoned the walker for a cane. Jackie asked him if he needed help. He took her arm to steady.

"After it's all burnt out?" Cassie said. "A week. Maybe two."

"Just in time for crappie season. I need my fishing back," he said to Jackie. She could smell the cigarettes on him, and it made her want one something fierce. "Fishing's all I got since my wife's gone and passed. I like to sit up on the dock and rest this ole leg and fish. Sometimes I take a little boat out." He touched Jackie's arm. "We never did have kids."

She looked at him, and said, "I'm sorry."

"At some point a man learns to let go of his regrets," he said. "This here lake's my life now."

Jackie thought of the fish without oxygen. Their slow, innocent movement beneath the surface. The old man's gimp leg. This infernal loneliness. Cassie climbed out of the water, and they inhaled the kerosene as it swirled in orange trails on the surface. She lit matches, tossed them out. Slowly the flower island roared into a blue bonfire. This was the warmest Jackie had felt all day; something finally had heated up inside her. They all watched until the hyacinth was completely engulfed, and Mr. Cecil grasped her hand and she felt so relieved to be out of prison, and back here that she gave his hand a squeeze, and then when the fire began to fade, Jackie eased Mr. Cecil into a wicker chaise. He got out his wallet and separated bills, licking his index finger and thumb. He kissed Cassie's forehead and thanked her. He whispered to Jackie for them to come fish with him some day. Jackie kissed his oily head and told him she would, though she knew that they'd never be back here again.

Jackie drove around to the other side of the lake. The old man's crippled figure hunched in the distance. "I don't know why he couldn't just light his own fire?" she asked.

"He wanted to do it hisself. It took months for him to understand how dangerous for a cripple to be climbing in the water with fire. I told him he'd light hisself on fire and then what good would it do him to be a floating dead man. The best part is he doesn't have anybody. I've been his family. A shame I won't see him again. I got attached."

Jackie imagined how Mr. Cecil would feel when those purple flowers bloomed. She hoped he didn't hate her; she hoped he could forgive her. The thought of his simple wish made Jackie want Cassie to hurt like that just to see what it was like. "Seems like a man that old would know better by now than to believe in a cheat like you."

Cassie just smiled, and Jackie knew Cassie had it in her to go on lying and thieving forever.

On the far end of the lake, lily pads coasted in patches so thick you could walk on them. "See them?" Cassie said.

White lilies opened into delicate palms, the white fingers curling skyward. Jackie was afraid to confess she thought them stunning. Perhaps she'd lost the ability to differentiate what was pretty and what wasn't. "I see them."

"That's our next project. Course we can't come back here, but there's plenty to go around. We'll get us a hand till. Then we'll go telling people how invasive the stuff is, how it will fill up the whole lake. How it will take over the world."

Jackie was catching on to Cassie's work now. "But it really won't?"

Cassie laughed so hard she snorted through her nose. "No!" she said.

Jackie waited for her to finish the story. "We'll grind them up and those little legs will multiply and shoot down to the bottom of the lake and root. Just like a star fish. You heard the story Daddy told of them crabbers thinking star fish were menacing—pulling off legs, thinking they'd killed them?" She paused to catch her breath again. "The starfish had the last laugh. They just grew a leg back in its place and that new leg made a new starfish! Same here. We'll till up the lilies and they'll multiply. I feel like I've got some great part in the world now, like I'm spreading my own seeds."

IN ALL, THEY POCKETED TWO HUNDRED bucks. Cassie knew a Tallahassee nursery that would give a hundred a piece for those sago palms. Cassie let Jackie off at Tim's Fast Nickel in Micanopy. She'd stalk the streets for new places to release flies, then when it got good and dark, she'd come for her, and they'd creep through lawns to liberate them. Cassie drove off giddy and whistling.

At Tim's Fast Nickel, Jackie bought a double cone of Rocky Road and Mississippi Mud. She walked down the lanes of antique shops and used record stores. She stared at her reflection and wondered when her eyes had grown dark like her sister's. She rested on a bench and watched Christmas shoppers maneuver bags. The sun was setting, melting the Spanish moss in the water oaks a mournful tangerine. Here she was in the wide open. She could do anything. She could buy another double cone of ice cream. Pistachio, superman, lime sherbet. This was how it felt to be alive. She wished Quinta was here. She'd type a letter for her soon. Cassie screeched to the curb, pressed on the horn. "Hurry!" she called. "They're on to us."

They sped down lake roads, branches scuffing metal. The Sagos slid from their pots. A stolen hand tiller bounced between the shovels. Jackie's hands shook so she gripped the door handle. She watched the rear view for blue lights. She'd been out two days. She couldn't lose her freedom now.

"I think I heard a siren," Jackie said. They neared Hawthorne Road, and a deer leaped from the tangly brush. Jackie screamed. Cassie slowed, then drove off the road, ploughed a plot of weeds and saplings. The Custom Deluxe lounged half in and out of the woods. Cassie stretched over Jackie for the Pall Malls in the glove compartment

"What the hell are you doing?" Jackie said. She listened for a siren.

"Got a secret, Jack." Cassie lit a cigarette. "I was lying back there. Nobody's after us."

"I'm getting out," Jackie said. The door caught on a cedar bough. She squeezed past it.

"I was only joking," Cassie said. "We got work to do, flies to let go."

"Damn you," Jackie yelled. The night was cloudy, the moonlight muted and soft. Jackie ran.

"We got devastation to cultivate," Cassie called.

There she was with those big words again, Jackie thought. She squatted to catch her breath. *Devastation. Cultivate.* If she went any further all crazy without direction she'd be lost. Cassie called again, her voice all sing-song. Proof, Jackie thought, she'd never seen life through razor wire. Quinta's voice was far away. Jackie tried to conjure it. Go, little mama, go. Typing music and playing words? Could they ever be the same? Maybe the things she and Quinta had said in their cell were only meant to move them through darkness.

The truck started up. Jackie turned back; she punctured through spider web traps. Cassie was capable of leaving her. Her own sister would do that. Jackie wanted freedom even if it meant cheating people. But she wouldn't do it forever, not like Cassie. She wrestled the cloying string from her hair, brushed off its plump maker, a banana spider that pinched the soft skin of her hand. Jackie remembered a time when they were kids and she and Cassie set up target practice in the piney woods. They'd shot those fat yellow and black-spotted spider bodies full of bb's, an act that Jackie now remembered as both barbaric and gratifying.

"Cassie," Jackie yelled. "Wait."

The engine revved in response; headlights punctured the weeds and flamed a white path to the truck.

King of the Mountain

TO RUN THE DEVIL CHILDREN OF Camp Good News off his property, Billy Durden rescued four bullhorns from the high school football stadium's demolition; he situated them in bald pines at Lake Nelle's jungled edge. The megaphones were as enormous as Brahman ears. Their pink enamel, once glossy as conch shell apertures, was now lackluster, smelted by the Florida sun. When wind bugled through, there was no islander's proclamation, instead an ominous revival of Friday nights past—a press box play-by-play, furious pom-poms and thirty-yard hail Marys, sorcerous majorettes, a trumpeter's battle cry. Billy found these phantom broadcasts oddly comforting.

It took three days to run cables from the trees to the cabin on stilts. Billy dug deep trenches, sunk the line in PVC conduit and coaxed it through a hole in the kitchen floor to a pawn-shop PA system on the kitchen table. The ancient console had a 35w rms amplifier and a single paging microphone. When he flipped the switch, and said, "Hello?" his voice sparked, then fizzled out.

For weeks those kids-turned-pirates had pilfered his storage shed and scrap pile, engineered ramshackle hideouts with their copped riches. Billy tried everything—he arranged saw-horse barricades, posted NO TRESPASSING signs, strung yellow police tape. He rejected over-priced estimates of cedar dog-ear plank fences and flimsy hardware-store pickets. Camp Good News was a sprawling acreage of aluminum-sided chapels—part holiness revival, part after-school ministry. On Monday, he marched over there to complain;

all he got was an invitation to lake-front vespers. The preacher, a self-proclaimed apostle, and his long-haired, stoic wife had at least a dozen children, all boys. Nobody needed that many kids, Billy thought. It just wasn't right. At this point, the older ones had surely grown up to have families of their own. Hellfire, these ones looting his property could be the preacher's *grandkids*.

Billy adjusted loose knobs and frayed wires. "Hello," he called. His voice thundered godlike over hundred-year-old palms and oaks teaming with Spanish moss. He shut off the microphone and grinned. He'd teach the little scoundrels a lesson. The very second they stepped onto his land, he'd holler them off; they'd think they were hearing a voice from the heavens.

SMITH BROTHERS HARDWARE DELIVERED a 12-foot heap of commercial sand that sparkled like quartz. Billy admired it from the kitchen table over his lunch of deep-fried okra peppered in cornmeal, a mess of pink-eyed purple hull peas from his last trip to Alabama, and an icy longneck of dark lager. As always, he had the day planned. He'd groom the sand with an aluminum-tined rake, arrange plastic Adirondacks to face the water. He set the dishes in the sink, and imagined a hammock nap and tangy breezes. Outside, voices called, "King of the Mountain, King of the Mountain." He scrambled to the window. It was *them*. The Camp Good News kids. They pawed to the peak. Filthy footprints tracked the sand. *His* sand. Billy upended his beer getting to the microphone. He flipped the switch. "Get offa my sand."

The raggedy kids became freeze-tag statues. Their eyes searched for the voice's origin.

"Get off now."

Billy listened in wonder as his words ricocheted from the opposite shore. The kids looked across the glinting lake to the beach strewn with outcast rowboats, rusty-laddered floating docks, and lopsided, gangly piers. It was as if his own voice, penned up inside worn-out trailers, was now liberated and shouting back at him from the open jalousie windows.

The tallest boy, a shirtless urchin, seemed to realize that regardless the source of the voice, he ought to be terrified. He ran for the water like an animated character, arms and knees pumping until all but his tow head disappeared beneath the surface. The other two raced home, taking the footpath behind Billy's cabin. That left the fourth, the skinniest of all, undoubtedly so fearful he couldn't move. Billy felt a jolt of pity toward the little fellow. He knew what it was like to be left behind. He spoke into the microphone, his voice soft. "Go on like the rest of them. You hear?"

The boy crossed his arms.

"Hey," Billy said. This was supposed to be easy. He'd shout commands into the PA; they'd obey.

The kid reared his right leg back and kicked. White granules spewed. He kicked again and again. Billy shut off the microphone, and ran downstairs.

The child was giggling, a pretty, singsong melody. Billy stepped closer. This kid he'd believed to be a boy with stringy clipped hair and mismatched clothes was a girl. From the top of the sand pile, she glared with sickly gray eyes, daring him to come closer.

"You," he said. "This is private property."

She balled her fists, and Billy braced. Rubber band bracelets cuffed her thin wrists. Her knees were knobby bones. Did the preacher make them go out on their own and scavenge? Once when he was a boy in Castleberry, Alabama, a man broke into their shed and stole canned green beans and scuppernong preserves. Instead of calling the sheriff, his mother set out plates of hot collard greens and fatback, bricks of buttered cornbread. Billy always wished he'd favored his mother. He looked toward the house. There were plenty of leftovers. He should leave a jar of chocolate milk, too. He was thinking of how he'd balance the meal on the mess of firewood the kids had rummaged through the day before, when a blast of sand struck him across his cheek. Fistfuls came with alarming speed.

"Stop. Stop," Billy said. He spat and wiped grit from his eyes.

She took off in a nonchalant stride. Billy swallowed and sand crunched against his back molars.

A BARBED-WIRE FENCE KNITTED with confederate jasmine divided Billy's property from Camp Good News. He eased through a narrow opening to find the preacher tending raised beds made of steel rebar and freshly planed two-by-fours. Bulging tomatoes listed off their vines, but the okra had bolted into six-foot stalks of dainty white flowers. It was a real shame, Billy thought. A careless waste. All it took to prevent a crop from going to seed was harvesting once or twice a week, and mulching to keep the ground cool. When the preacher offered his hand, Billy plunged his palms into his back pockets.

"You know that okry is inedible." He heard himself say *okry* like his grandmother used to say, but he couldn't bring himself to correct it.

The preacher collected a full basket, husks dark green and woody. Billy nodded toward the spent crop.

"You won't be able to eat it. You neglected them so long, the plant used all its energy making seeds. Survival mode is what they call it."

The preacher picked up one of the okra pods, and took a bite. He chewed with wide eyes and spit out what he couldn't swallow. He grinned.

"You come all the way over here to tell me how to keep my garden?"

"I come over here to tell you what them kids did to my brand-new sand."

There was the grin again; it made Billy feel petty. The preacher was shirtless. A gray ponytail fell down his back. Plaid Bermuda shorts slung off his gaunt frame, and he wore braided flip-flops. Caribbean wear, Billy thought, not preacher attire. It was that year-long mission trip that made him grow his hair long and dress like a bum. "Since you come back from the islands, they running loose, and taking my things. I won't have it."

"Your speakers gave them a real scare."

"They been asking for it. I told you last time—"

The preacher leaned close. "Is it godly?"

Billy thought he didn't hear him right. "Godly?"

The preacher nodded. "Yes."

"Is pestering the life out of someone godly?" He waited for the preacher to answer, but he carried on with his weeding.

"Them kids wreaked havoc on my sour plums. Last week, I found my best canoe dragged up on that floating dock out yonder." Billy pointed toward the lake at the play forts that resembled hobbit houses and duck blinds. "The mess they've made—" The preacher's back was to him, and Billy felt his face flush. He didn't like being ignored. "If I'm not godly enough, you report me and my speakers to the police."

The preacher yanked on a potato vine. "These things are awful invasive."

"You need to pull up all the tubers, and then burn them." Billy felt smug. "They'll grow eight inches a night if you let them."

It took the preacher two tries with both hands to get the soft-ball sized root out of the soil. He held it high like a trophy rattler, the tendrils hanging three feet. He looked to Billy, and winked. "Survival mode."

Billy frowned and looked toward movement in the deep shade of the live oaks. One of the kids dashed beneath the low-hanging branches, vanished behind a large structure flanked by aluminum storage sheds. The prefabricated buildings were painted white with blue trim, and even from here the paint looked glossy and fresh. Tacked over the main door was a varnished cypress cross. In the distant, darkened plot of the trees was a treasure trove of castoff playground equipment — a rocket slide, a witch's hat with a wooden foothold, an assortment of animal springers mounted to the ground with rusty metal coils, their over-sized cartoon eyes paint-chipped. Beyond that, there was a climbing wall, rope swings, zip-lines, and an elaborate pirate ship tree house, and further on toward the shore, a water slide with a steep rickety ladder. Billy remembered seeing its name, the Living Water slide, in an advertisement for summer camp. The black plastic chute twisted a hundred feet to the lake.

"You got an amusement park back there. You think they'd never want to leave it to come mess with things at my property."

The preacher settled his hands in his pockets. "I'll talk with them," and then he went about with the weeds again. "I told you I would."

Billy detected a note of irritation in the preacher's voice. He was trying to tell Billy to go home, but Billy suddenly wasn't ready to go. He didn't like being told what to do.

"I thought you had all boys," Billy said.

"Excuse me?"

"Thought you had a dozen boys."

The preacher nodded. "Just about. We have ten."

"No girls?"

"We never were blessed with a girl child."

"No girl grandchildren?"

The preacher wiped his brow. "Like I said, all boys. Even the grandkids."

Billy couldn't believe the odds. All boys. How does something like that happen? "But who's the girl? She rurnt my sand. Kicked it at me. Kicked it all over. You shoulda seen it."

"That's Deedee. My wife's niece. Staying with us from Georgia."

"She's your ring leader."

"I don't doubt it. She's bad blood. A hard life in her eleven years. Looks like you got on her bad side."

The big sail on the treehouse ship bristled at intermittent gusts. The kid appeared again, and Billy was certain it wasn't the girl. This was one of the younger boys, playing hide and seek. His tow head would appear, then disappear. The preacher grinned, but Billy didn't like being fooled with.

"My bad side?" Billy said, suddenly concerned about someone taking advantage of him, teasing him. "What do you mean by that?"

"I'd watch my back if I were you," and then the preacher laughed. "I told her time's just about up. I told her, Deedee, you get in trouble again, we'll send you to reform school."

"Military school?"

The preacher shook his head. "Juvenile detention. Razor wire, the whole nine yards."

Deedee didn't seem like the type to let herself be contained. "What might become of a child—a girl—locked up like that?"

The preacher squinted at Billy. His tone was flippant. "I'll take care of her. You go on now." He nodded toward the big aluminum building, glowing white in the noon sun. "How about you come to chapel tomorrow? I think you could use some time with the Lord."

Billy studied the structure the preacher referred to as the chapel. It looked like a fancy carport for motor homes. The up and over doors were closed, and there were no windows. It reminded him of the dusty volunteer fire station that served as the makeshift Second Baptist Church when he was a kid growing up in Castleberry. Every Sunday morning, an old timer named Hank backed the truck out of the bay to make room for the congregation. Dried diesel fuel pooled beneath their folding chairs. All the years they attended, there never was a fire. It had been such a disappointment. They finally left Second Baptist for New Life Way, a Pentecostal church in Brewton, because Billy's sister, Maggie, and two neighborhood girls, accused the pastor of groping them. It was the beginning of his sister's decline. That's what time with the Lord had gotten his family.

"No, thank you," Billy said. "You can have the good Lord all to yourself."

THAT NIGHT, BILLY STARTED IN EARLIER than usual on the Jim Beam. He rigged a hammock on the deck, and closed his eyes to a breeze of water lilies and purple hyacinth. He fidgeted and fussed. That girl's stare had borne into him. He wondered if she slept at night. Maybe she walked the house, plotting destinies, oiling guns. What crime had gotten her into such trouble that her own family banished her? Before they left for the islands, those boys had been no trouble. In fact, they were hermit like. Was it the girl's influence? Did her meanness convert them to wickedness?

Billy turned his attention to the water. Lake Nelle was pretty, but only a fool would come back from the Caribbean for Hawthorne, Florida. What with all the world's problems? Crazy politics in your face all the damn time? Why wouldn't somebody stay over there where it seemed like the power was out half the time? Hell, that way you wouldn't know what was going on in the first place. And, the water? Lake Nelle was deep and spring fed, but he'd seen pictures of the translucent Caribbean, starfish burying themselves in the sand, arms outstretched, disappearing from the world.

Billy took a swig of Jim Beam. He could feel the anger building, anger at those kids, at the preacher's nonsense, at that age-old unidentified furor deep inside him. Tree frogs clacked an archaic marbled song. The louder their crescendo, the more it kept the rage at bay, so he drank and let the whiskey chorus lift him up. He imagined they were angels of some sort, not frogs. When the tidings receded, he waited almost breathless for them to start up again. Out of the corner of his eye, Billy glimpsed a black tendon gliding through the water. He directed his flashlight on an unintimidated snake, its body skating the water with precision, unhindered and heading straight for the beam of light.

At first, Billy assumed it was a harmless banded water snake, shiny and reflective in the moonlight, but this beast was dull with keeled scales and raised lines up and down its ropey body. Its head was so blocky, he couldn't make out the eyes. Billy couldn't remember the last time he'd seen a water moccasin on the lake. Hell, they were there, but they kept to themselves. Back home on the muddy Alabama, they were so prevalent there were stories of cottonmouths shimmying up pilings on long piers in search of revenge, as if they'd identified sunbathers and beer drinkers who deserved it. It was those aggressive serpents that made him into a high-school champion water skier. Once while treading in the blood orange river after taking a spill a moccasin chased him to the bank before his brother, Pete, could swing the Ski Nautique around to save him. Just before the snake lunged, Billy grabbed a low branch and jumped ashore. He developed superhuman balancing powers; he never fell again, and placed second and third at the Tallassee regionals two years in a row.

Billy kept the light pointed at the creature as he eased off the hammock. All these years, he'd managed to stay clear, but this one found him. With caution, Billy reached for the Jim Beam, but it rolled toward the ledge. The coiled snake opened its ivory mouth; it vibrated and hissed. Billy yelled like a sissy, and ran to the house without his liquor.

HE HAD A FITFUL NIGHT'S SLEEP thinking of the girl and the snake. He woke before dawn, grateful for the much-needed distraction a full day of physical labor would bring. It was only September, but the humidity of January and February in North Florida would turn the air bone cold. A wide, shallow fireplace was the cabin's only source of heat, and it was Billy's habit by early September to ready six cords of firewood for curing. He was already two weeks behind schedule. He blamed his tardiness on the time-consuming installation of the speakers and the PA system, and the extra attention his sandy beach had needed once those kids messed with the sand pile. Thankfully, he'd collected downed limbs all summer, and there was a stockpile of sweetgum, white oak, and cedar awaiting him in the clearing. If he got started now and worked all through the rest of the week, there would be plenty of time for it to fully season in the ventilated shed by the new year.

Burning green wood is bad luck and dangerous. When damp wood burns, the fire sputs and spurts and battles moisture instead of giving off a nice flame, a process that creates a flammable carbon called creosote. The fool who owned the cabin before him had undoubtedly been unaware of the tar-like layer of combustible residue building on the walls of the chimney. Gone unchecked, it's nearly impossible to remove. When Billy bought the cabin, he'd noticed the telling odor like that of a freshly paved asphalt driveway. It took buckets of vinegar to purge the noxious smell, and a professional chimney sweep to clean the upper walls of the fireplace.

By 9 o'clock, he'd made little progress. When he thought of the girl and what she might have done to be turned away from her family, a peculiar sadness filled him with dread, and the only thing that made it go away was raising the axe high above his head then coming down on a two-by-four of cedar. He did that one too many times, and suddenly felt his shoulder give.

In the distance, there was the off-beat knocking of hammers. He wished it was thunder, and sat down on a stump and listened long and hard until he finally decided it was the sound of iron on wood. He couldn't see where it was coming from. The sky had turned an angry shade of purple he'd not seen in a long time. It had been thundering for days, a deep rumbling and growling, a building hunger. But no rain. Earlier in the summer, just after Memorial Day, it had rained every day. It would grumble and clack around up there, until right on time, at 3:30 p.m., the bottom would fall out. He could set his watch by the afternoon storms. They were harmless, good old-fashioned downpours. Every few days there'd be a round of lightning that made the hair on his arm stand up straight. It would start far off over the other side of the lake, and inch its way close—these big dipper flashes in blue white. But now, come 5 p.m., and it hadn't rained, or even hinted at it going on six weeks. He'd been counting on a hard rain to pat down his sand, but there was nothing but an occasional darkening of the sky, a bout of wind, and then it would right itself, and the sun would come out. But always, in the background there was a faint thunderous bass, gearing up for something majestic.

Billy worked on through lunch. He stopped only to listen for the marching bands, the referee's whistle, but there was no wind, and no old dreams, only the far-off hammering that had now begun keeping time with his own. His throat was parched, and his whole body stiff, and he realized he'd not stopped for as much as a sip of water. Billy sat on the stump again, took a long drink from his thermos. He thought about the bottle of Jim Beam he'd lost the night before, the snake's arrowhead silhouette and slitted eyes. A child's voice interrupted him.

"Sir."

He turned to see the girl, Deedee.

"Sir," she said again. It wasn't a question. It was simply as if the child was pointing him out to someone as if that thing over here, she was saying, is a sir.

It seemed as if she had been crying until he realized she was streaked with mud, her hair dripping with duck weed and algae. She swung a hammer alongside her skinny legs.

"Go one more step," he said. "You get any closer, I'll call the preacher."

"I'm not on your property." She teased a foot over an imaginary line. "I'm standing off it. You're afraid of me."

"I'm not afraid of a kid. The preacher's sending you off if you and those boys don't leave me and my things alone. If I were you, I'd behave for now."

She nodded, neither concerned nor impressed. "Why? Why are you afraid?"

Her very presence struck a deep, deep chord, and that confused him.

"That question doesn't deserve an answer." He picked up his axe, and despite the growing numbness in his biceps, let it come crashing down on the thick hardwood, splintering it into a satisfying log, perfect for the fireplace. After a while, she got bored, and walked away, back toward the Living Water slide. The hammering started up again, and now something had changed in the atmosphere. He could decipher its origin, along the shore. He squinted toward the water slide and saw the girl's figure, her own actions mimicking his—hammer raised above her head, pelting wood and God only knows what else. Long as it wasn't his things she was tearing apart he didn't care what the little hellion did. Let her take her meanness out on something and somebody else.

Billy continued on another hour, arranging tidy rows of wood. He studied his hard work, exhausted, but proud, and then hobbled to the house. The front room was baking from the afternoon sun, but he was so tired, he left the windows open. Just before he collapsed on the sofa, he set out hamburger meat to thaw; he hadn't eaten a thing all day.

Billy woke, disoriented, to a gray-brown sky and distant chanting. Had he slept through the night? The icepack under his throbbing back was warm. He studied the lake and the light, and listened to the song of the red birds. It was a female's evening call to her mate, summoning him to bring food home to the nest. He'd slept till dinner time. Smoke from a faraway brush fire filled the air. It had still not rained.

He opened the door, strained to hear the voices that came from the speakers. The ball was on the five-yard line. Cheerleaders worked their mantra. *Push it, push it, push it cross that line. Hey.* There were shouts, screams. A whistle blew. The crowd broke into a deep groan. *Off sides,* the referee called. *Ball goes to Ochwilla.* The crowd booed, heartbroken. Billy winced at the official's bad call, the stinging in the muscles of his upper back, but suddenly was renewed at the thought of the wood he'd cut and stacked neatly at the edge of the storage shed. Tomorrow, if he was able, he'd start in on another cord.

Suddenly starving, Billy worked the thawed hamburger into a thick patty, set it under the broiler, heated up peas with salty pork and black pepper like his grandmother always did. He'd bought them the month before at the crossroads vegetable stand in Ollie, Alabama, on his way to Castleberry to his sister's funeral. He'd not thought of that vegetable stand in years, but as soon as he got off the interstate in Milton and drove across the state line at Dixon, he was deep in pea country. Field after field of the pretty speckled ladies, crowders, creamers, pink-eye purple hulls. He'd gotten to thinking about lunch at his grandmother's, about those days when things were still right and good, and the car practically drove itself to the little produce stand, and he'd bought up all they had—twenty-four bags. At a family-owned hardware store, he bought an enormous Igloo cooler meant for catfish fillets, stacked the quart bags on a ten-pound bag of ice, then turned around and drove straight back to Florida. Every time he looked at his funeral suit swaying from the back-seat hook, he directed his thoughts to the peas and how good they'd taste after simmering all day. When he got home, there were eight voice mails from his brother. He listened to the words—a tangle of disbelief and rage that he'd not come to the service—and then hit the delete button.

Billy spooned up a bowl of peas, and sipped the broth. He added a dash of salt, and thought of that little girl, Deedee. Could she see into his heart? What *was* he afraid of? He just wanted to be left alone. That was all. The hamburger popped and sizzled under the broiler. Usually, he loved the smell of a good hamburger, but today the greasy mess was nauseating. He thought of Maggie and how after she and the others accused the fire station pastor of touching them and whispering crude jokes, something changed about her. Throughout her childhood, she'd been quiet and introverted, almost stone faced. Suddenly, she shunned friends for dropouts who cruised the town square in souped-up trucks. She'd disappear for days at a time, sending their mother into fits. Eventually, she quit school. When their father died, and Pete went off to the Army, their mother hardly could keep track of Maggie. Billy wanted to right things, to please his mother. Out of desperation, he recruited dates for his sister, promising them his hard-earned cash. But, he couldn't find a soul—none of his decent friends—to take him up on it.

Billy went to the window and stared across the lake toward the house trailers, forgotten jon boats, unkempt chain-link fences and dog pens. He remembered the morning his mother woke him to say Maggie was south of town at the county line, that she'd taken up with a gang living in an abandoned hunting cabin. Billy drove his father's pickup along mauled curtains of kudzu, great walls that grew darker and darker as if he were driving into a tunnel. His pickup skidded on red-dirt lanes. Blackberry vines climbed telephone poles. His sister was there with three boys. They stood on the leaning front porch and teased Billy. He squirmed against the pickup. His hands shook.

"Go home, Billy," Maggie said from the doorway.

"But, Mama—"

"But, *Mama*," the boys mimicked in chorus.

Billy shoved them aside. The boys swatted him like an old dog.

One of them goosed him and Maggie laughed.

He felt childish as he told the boys, "I'm not leaving without my sister." He turned to her, but was repulsed by her coy grin, the threadbare dress above her knees. "I want to help."

She came closer and smiled.

He thought he'd convinced her. "Come on, now. Get your things," he said.

The smile vanished. "You going to pay them, too?"

That got a rile out of the boys. One said, "I sure wish you would, big brother."

Billy tried to explain. "I meant good by it. Listen—"

"I do what I please." She shut the door in his face.

He'd lied to his mother, said she wasn't there. A few weeks later, out of the blue, Maggie ran off with another boy, the Ratner's oldest. They settled out west. There were rumors she was pregnant, and that was why she'd run off, but she never did have children, and she didn't return, not even for their mother's funeral. He never saw her again. All those years, he was relieved she'd never returned. It wasn't until she died four months ago and his brother had her body sent back to Alabama on the train that she finally did come home.

Billy crumbled cornbread into his peas. Why had he even started the burger? He turned off the oven, wrapped the uneaten patty in tin foil. He picked at the peas. He'd lost his appetite. All of this because of a little girl who looked nothing like his sister. Maggie had long, red hair, haughty blue eyes. Deedee was a forgotten waif. He needed a drink. He took down a glass from the cabinet, reached for his bottle on the back shelf of the pantry. It was gone.

The dock, he remembered. He'd left it there the night before. Billy put on a T-shirt, and headed down to the water. Remembering the snake, he hesitated, and surveyed the wide planks. The hammock shook with a hot breeze. He bent to check the dock's underside where fire ants burrowed and green anoles scurried in leaf litter. His flip flops were where he'd left them—the whiskey, gone.

BILLY SLEPT LATE THE NEXT MORNING. After eating an omelet with cheddar and tomatoes, he felt better than he had in days. His shoulder was only slightly sore, and he'd not woken at all during the night thinking of that feral child, or his lost sister for that matter. And, there'd been little carrying on from the camp kids. The PA system had been a good deterrent, certainly worth the hassle. If he was lucky, the little girl was gone for good. Maybe the preacher had shipped her off and Billy would never have to see her again. He took his time getting outside to the firewood, making phone calls, and balancing his checkbook. His social security check had come the week before, and he was pleased to see he had a little leftover—some funny money, as his grandmother used to call it—after paying the bills. Maybe he'd buy a striped umbrella for his sandy beach.

By the time he got down to the clearing, Billy was in such good spirits it took a minute to realize not one piece of the wood he'd left the day before in methodically arranged stacks was there. He turned his head in disbelief from one side of the yard to the next, aware he looked like those kids when he hollered at them from the microphone. He recalled the incessant drumming the day before, Deedee's sudden appearance, her questioning, that hammer slinging at her side.

"Damn," he said. "Goddamn."

Billy took off toward the Living Water slide. From a distance, the structure seemed sturdy and well-constructed. Now, he could see the spongy trestle was rotted and its splintered ladder missing all but the top rungs. On the ground was a plywood sign undoubtedly yanked from the broad wall. Billy looked to his cabin and back along the shoreline, and thought about all the ruckus from yesterday. That girl. That girl had hammer clawed the nails from the ladder rungs, then clubbed them into the hand painted letters. He imagined what the preacher might do when he discovered the destruction. Billy could still make out the punctured words: "He that believeth, out of his belly shall flow rivers of living water, John 7:38."

Billy thought back to the fire station of his churching days, the sermons that left him hollow and afraid. Living water. Eternal life. A cold needling pricked his hands. The girl had a dark meanness in her, and it scared Billy that he recognized it. There, in the distance, a flag made of ragged flowery sheets pulsed in the wind. He walked through debris and wood scraps to the shore. The pitiful flag was secured to a broomstick and then to an elaborate vessel, a sturdy raft of wide plywood planks and logs, *Billy's* logs. Stacked on a two-by-four shelf were T-shirts and pants, cans of white beans and sweet corn. His whiskey bottle was latched to the prow like a figurehead. It spilled speckled killifish and lake water. He found the hammer and ripped the makeshift boom apart until his own wood was nothing but kindling. He grabbed the bottle by the neck, and took off for the preacher's house. He pounded the door with his fist. There was no answer. From the aluminum shed an out-of-tune piano with sticky keys played "Shall We Gather at the River." Billy flung open the door.

Thirty or forty men and women watched from aluminum folding chairs; children screamed. Women rocked their babies and turned their soft faces from him. Was it Sunday morning? He had lost track of the days. Deedee and the boys sat, hands folded, with pious expressions, as if they didn't know him.

He held his bottle high. "I want my whiskey back. I want that wood."

The preacher walked from the pulpit, a sad podium of particle board and veneer. He motioned Billy to go outside. A light rain ticked the tin roof.

"You ought not to come in like that. You scared my congregation."

"Come look at what she's done." Billy pointed toward the mess strewn along the shore. He took the preacher's arm. "The girl—"

With a practiced gesture, the preacher reached into his pocket, held out a fifty-dollar bill.

"Is that from the offering plate?" Billy said. "I don't want God's money. I want them kids gone."

The preacher frowned. "You should seek help."

A warm drizzle fell on their hands and faces. Billy said, "Get my things back."

The preacher put the fifty back in his pocket. "It's going to storm. We'll see to that later." He touched Billy's elbow. "You don't look well."

Billy listened for the cheerleaders, the quarterback signaling his receiver, and the whale-bellowing tuba, but he was all alone. He approached the defunct Living Water slide, and the compromised vessel. Over his shoulder, he yelled to the preacher, "I better not see them kids on my property ever again."

By the time he got to the lake, the congregation had commenced with their old-timey hymns. He knew the words by heart, and soon he was longing for bloody lambs and rugged crosses. The preacher had surely dead-bolted the door on him. Billy walked the shore, and discovered stolen items from his shed: a chain saw, a gas can, a broken pressure washer wand. He carted them in a wobbly wheelbarrow and then rolled a lawnmower tire with his good arm. He heated leftover peas and ate them straight from the pan. He swallowed Ibuprofen with a cold beer chaser.

BY MIDNIGHT, THE LIGHT RAIN WAS a downpour. Billy was bone tired, but the raging storm kept him from sleep. He crept out of bed with a fleece blanket. Blue-white flashes set the water on fire. Just as the snake had done, the lightning took its time coming for him. As if he could hide from such a thing, Billy crouched on the floor, and wondered if he had gone to the funeral, if he had owned up to Pete, would that girl still be haunting him? If Deedee hadn't taken over his sand pile, would he have even thought of his dead sister? All that hollering and elbowing to the top, vying for King of the Mountain. How Deedee pushed and shoved and kicked and hollered. Who did she think she was?

The storm brought a cold front. Billy wrapped the blanket around his shoulders. He remembered that hilltop game in Alabama, being tackled by Pete, vying for the king himself. But back home, those hills were of sawdust, not sand—great big piles of sawdust his daddy brought from the pulp mill to sell. Billy remembered how he and Pete shoveled from the bed of the pickup. Sometimes the wood shavings were still smoking from the baling machine. They'd watch as the wind flamed embers, and then gleefully stomp them out. He hadn't thought of that in years, how the heat warmed the soles of his cheap boots. One morning a dump truck arrived with the biggest mountain they'd seen in their lives. Maggie was there too. She'd fought her way to the top, and as they all loved to do, dropped into the hill pretending they were jumping off Red Eagle's bluff. That was when the screaming began. First, he'd thought it was because she couldn't breathe and had panicked, and then he'd smelled smoke. It was Pete who realized an ember in the hill's belly had sparked the white cotton of Maggie's gown. Billy watched, helpless. Pete knocked her to the ground, rolling out flames. Maggie's hair and her gown's hem were singed.

Outside, lightning knifed the sky revealing Lake Nelle as a quivering pool of heat. Thunder boomed, a wicked bolt followed, and Billy ducked as if a comet had been hurled at him. The lightning was desperate for something to grab hold of and bring down. He tried to remember the rules of grounding. Did you take hold of something wooden or rubber? Were you to stay away from the shore where water met land? Or was it the center of the body of water that was most dangerous? Deedee had been right. He *was* deathly afraid. He picked up the landline on the coffee table, dialed his brother's number. He'd tell Pete why he didn't attend the funeral. Even in death, he couldn't face his sister. He was a coward. He would always be a coward. Wasn't that easy to understand?

"Billy?" Pete picked up on the second ring. In his voice, there was brotherly concern and confusion. "Billy? Is that you?"

A flash illuminated the raised scales of a live oak. Billy recalled the story of an old woman talking to her son on the phone. Lightning traveled up the line. She went deaf in her left ear.

"Billy?" Pete was saying. "What's wrong?" There was another strike; Billy dropped the receiver.

Outside there was a debilitating hush as if all violence had ceased. The phone rang and rang. Billy eased up, his hand on the window sill. If he was motionless and quiet, or prayed, maybe evil would forget him. He closed his eyes and pretended to ask the Lord for help. A crack leapt from the sky like fangs, and everything went cottonmouth white; Billy fell to the floor, and there was the hissing of a flame chasing possibilities, searching for what it wanted. The phone rang on and on. Pete was a good brother; he wouldn't give up. Billy felt heat chasing beneath the floorboards and along baseboards, and inside the wall and into the TV and the refrigerator and stove until it had taken everything he had, everything it needed. The ringing phone went silent.

Billy fell asleep on the floor and awoke to a foreboding stillness, the odor of burning plastic; the ceiling fan, motionless; the appliances, soundless. His feet were hot. He wiggled his toes. He'd dreamed of the sawdust pile. An osprey at the top of a palm tree balked. Billy checked the fuse box. The main breaker had tripped, and when he flipped it back, there was nothing.

He went outside to investigate. The wood was where he'd left it the night before, organized in neat bundles beneath the tarp. The air reeked of hot wiring. The ground where the wires were buried steamed. Undoubtedly, the lightning had found its way into the cabin through the cables that circled the trees and fed his PA system and ghost speakers. The megaphones in the trees, no longer portals of the past, sat drooping, ashamed.

The soaking rain had woken the resurrection ferns; their spines unfurled along dented oak arms. Over his property line, almost out of ear shot, the boys from Camp Good News spun the witch's hat. Billy searched for Deedee's fierce figure. Did the preacher send her away? He thought of the ruined raft, her botched escape. The bullhorns were damned; there was nothing left to say. He raised his good arm. The dizzy boys climbed onto the bow of the pirate ship, as if casting off for good.

Like She Stole It

SOON AS DARCY SKIPPED OUT ON THE RENT, her landlord chain-sawed fifty feet of overgrown bay laurel from the lakefront cottage, exposing wide-eyed windows and a long-neglected leaning porch, allowing me ample views of my guilt. All that brush-hogging opened up the sound barrier, too. Truckers boom around the county road, headlights jetting diamonds to water. Yesterday, Stan said a woman was at the shop asking about me. "Tell Ray Darcy's back," she said, and I haven't thought about much else since. I got up before daylight, drank my Folgers Instant at the window, and each time those lights darted, I jumped. What this means, I decided, is I'm finally going to get what I deserve.

Out here on Lake Nelle, we're like family, especially the four of us on the western shore. Nobody knows my past, nobody knows their future; we all work together. This winter was a cold one in North Florida. Lots of frozen pipes, fallen branches, power outages. Just yesterday, my water pump died, and Cassius from the concrete block cottage on the corner brought a capacitor and my buddy Jake from next door installed it; I had running water in fifteen minutes. The old lady in the woods behind me, I help with her chickens. Last month, I built an ante room on the main coop, so she keeps me in organic free range—not that at my age and health it matters.

Last night, the temperature dipped to 34 degrees. There's no heat in here, so this morning I cranked the electric oven to 400, opened the door, ate my Quaker Oats wearing faded thermals, an orange hunting cap. I remembered the time there was a spring nor'easter and temperatures plummeted, roads flooded and Darcy rowed over in a battered Old Town canoe to spend the weekend. That was the first time we slept together, and after that we kept it up, didn't matter the weather. She'd come on Fridays after work, and Sunday night say, "It's time to go when the wine bottle's empty." Ole Jake and I would wink at each other because we went through a fifth of whiskey every night. I liked that about Darcy, how she was so fragile and delicate.

But things change. I made another mug of Folgers, waited for sunrise, imagined whiskey on my throat. It's been long days since I drank that way and tell you what, I can't make out whether it's a good thing or not. This old cabin sits on stilts, the only one like it at the lake. I prefer looking down on the lake, eye to eye with cardinals and acrobatic squirrels. The perspective suits me. I watched until the sun illuminated Darcy's side of the lake—I still think of it like that—*her* side. Before I knew it, the cabin was warm, too, just in time to get in my cold truck and head to work.

NOON TO ONE, MONDAY THROUGH FRIDAY, Stan has the daily special at Angel's Diner. Darcy rolled into the lot in a blue Ford Taurus as Stan drove off. She stood, hands on hips casing St. Johns Avenue. I'd imagined an awkward reunion, wondered if she'd ask to stay with me, if she'd want a hug. Soon as she started for the door, those tight Levi's, dainty hip sway, same old hair toss, were a knife to my gut, and I realized nothing much had changed; I'd do whatever it was she said.

The bells on the door bounced against Darcy's back. She called out, "Hey."

As I walked from around the counter, she planted her hands in her back pockets; affection wasn't what she needed. I was disappointed.

"Hey," I said. "Good to see you."

"Is it?" She laughed, and I was nervous, so I laughed, too. There was something different. Sure, there was the same old wispy way her arms moved, but there was a strange huskiness and irreverence in her voice, as if in the past year, she'd taken to smoking and thieving. There was nothing fragile about her.

"Listen, Ray," she said, talking like we'd seen each other the night before. "I need keys." She pointed at the assortment on the wall.

"Give me something that works. Nothing too shabby, nothing too shiny."

"What's this about?"

"I said I need a car. Your boss will be gone till one on the dot. Hurry."

I looked out back for Emmet, the contracted mechanic. He was under a truck. All I could see of him was his boots. "How do you know Stan's schedule?"

"Never mind that, damn it. Give me a car, and I'll have it back at five of."

"Look, I don't have that kind of authority. I answer the phone, run the register. I don't even know what he wants to work on next."

"I don't care *what* you do. I need them keys."

Two years ago when Darcy left, I was working in Keystone Heights, not far from Hawthorne. How she found me in Palatka, thirty miles away, made me uneasy.

"What kind of trouble you got yourself into, Darcy?"

"Bet you'd like to know."

There was that wicked grin of hers, the kind she used when we'd play Spades and she had the upper hand. I couldn't compete, so I turned to the peg board of keys. There were a dozen cars on the lot in various stages of disrepair. The Pontiac was the last to come in, so I handed her those, watched like a helpless fool as she took the car without so much as a nod goodbye. I stood there just as my grandpa and I watched my own mother drive away many times. She'd take his old Ford pickup, red dust flying down South Alabama roads. I was five or six, and from the front yard, I'd sob wondering if this would be the last time I'd ever see her. Grandpa would squeeze my hand, whisper, "Don't worry, son," then under his breath when the truck was out of sight, "She drove it like she stole it."

I SAT ON THE EDGE OF MY SEAT WONDERING what I'd tell Stan when he discovered that car gone. I couldn't imagine what Darcy needed it for. After a while, I went out to the Taurus, opened the door, expecting her scent—laundered clothes, lemons, sweet lavender. But it was all cigarettes and mildew. I opened the glove box. No registration. Ran my hand under the driver's seat. Not even an empty cigarette pack. I went back inside and paced.

Ten minutes to one when Emmett came to have coffee and shoot the bull, Darcy reappeared, parked the Pontiac under a shedding sycamore. Emmett stood to watch her prance toward the shop.

"Who we got here?" he asked, whistling. "Want me to see to her?"

"I'll take care of it."

"No fair."

I met Darcy halfway. She dangled the keys. I snatched them away. "Be discreet, will you?" I glanced toward the shop. Emmett waved. Darcy waved back. "Are you out of your mind?" I said. "I could lose my job. I'm good mind to call the police."

"You owe me—"

"I don't owe you a thing. I don't know what I was even thinking, giving in to you. You made your point, okay? I'm sorry about what happened to Will, but I don't know what else to do."

"Tell me," she said, grabbing my arms. "Why? Why did you do it?"

"We've been over this, Darce. I gave him money to get a fix. I never thought it'd end up like it did."

She let go, gave me the most hateful look. If you found a place in the sun, you could warm up, but we were both situated on the shady side of the building. Darcy shivered and it was all I could do not to embrace her. Her eyes were teary; she wiped her face with her sweatshirt sleeve.

"I was just trying to help."

"Well, you didn't. Do a better job at it next time." She wiped her eyes again, gathered herself. "I need another car, and I need it tomorrow at noon. Soon as your boss is gone. Don't let me down."

Just then Stan pulled into the lot, stopped the truck, rolled down the window.

"Hi-dy," he said, and then to Darcy. "See you found your friend."

"Yes sir, I did." She sounded sweet and chipper as could be.

"Well," he said, hesitating until it was awkward. "Nice to see you folks."

I turned to leave, and Darcy pinched my elbow. "Don't let me down."

Stan went upstairs to his office, but Emmett waited, poured himself another coffee. "You want to tell me about this?"

"No," I said, my back to him. "I don't." I pretended to read the *Palatka Daily News*, flipping pages back and forth. I didn't put the keys on the hook until Emmett had disappeared under another car.

AT SUNDOWN, WEARING A DOWN VEST, I took Darcy's Old
Town to the middle of the lake, drifted until the shore darkened, cabin
lights blinking on like fireflies. I thought of the first time Darcy's son,
Will, came to the lake, first time she'd seen him in seventeen years.
He was doing drugs, and his grandparents kicked him out. For years
he'd lived with Darcy's folks, various aunts and uncles, but she'd
never mentioned a word to me about having a son. I swear to God
one morning, I was on the water looking toward the shore and the
two of them side by side looked like brother and sister.

Now that he was in town, she'd made her mind up to save him, and
in hindsight I wonder if she hoped to redeem herself in the process.
She wanted me to talk sense into him, and I remember thinking it's a
little too late, but I went ahead and bought night crawlers and grass
shrimp, loaded the Igloo with cold Busch. Somehow I managed to
get Will out in the Old Town with a fishing pole. It was bream season,
and I was good at it, still am. Most seasons I'm over my limit starting
Memorial Day. I rowed to the center of the lake, then a hair toward
the northeast corner. "This is my lucky spot."

"Listen, Ray, my main man," Will said. "Thanks for playing this.
I just need to score some dope."

I wasn't a user anymore, got out of that years back. The stuff
took a decade off my life and my liver. I had a hard time finding my
way home. "Look, I told your mom I'd bring you fishing. We don't
need to talk about—"

"Stop calling her my mom. She's not a mom. She left me with her
mother. That's who I call *mom*."

"Hush now. Quiet down." Lake Nelle worked two ways: It could
swallow whatever you said, make it vanish forever, or there were days
every word Jake and Cassious said to each other from the jon boat
were enunciated like a school teacher's. I had no way of knowing
what kind of day this was shaping up to be, and I didn't want Darcy
hearing something she shouldn't. "You're a bitter young man."

"Wouldn't you be?"

I considered being honest, but settled on a half truth. "Son, we all
have things we're mad at. You got to learn to live with them."

"Wisdom. She sent me out here for wisdom."

"Earned it the hard way," I said, telling myself if he asked how, I'd tell him, but I wouldn't volunteer.

Will had Darcy's sharp chin, gray-blue eyes. He also had the stubborn anger that brewed up in her from time to time. It was hard not to stare at him. He must have been reading my mind. "All we share are genes. Far as I'm concerned."

After a while, I reeled in my line, rowed to shore.

WHEN SHE CAME INTO STAN'S the next day, we didn't speak. I handed her keys to a ten-year-old Honda Accord with an oil leak, a faulty valve cover. Ten minutes later, Emmett asked for the same car, and I said, "Not here."

He looked at his clipboard, then out at the lot. "This clipboard says it is."

"Well, it's wrong. Changed their minds."

I went back to the *Palatka Daily News*. This time Darcy didn't come in to talk, just left the keys in the car. When Emmet broke for coffee, there was the green Honda in the parking lot, plain as day.

"Changed their minds again?" he said, smirking.

"What it looks like."

THREE DAYS PASSED, AND DARCY didn't return. It became harder to face that cottage. I decided to escape Hawthorne a few days, clear my mind, flee the lake and any more requests from Darcy. In the meantime, if she returned, I'd tell her this game was over—no more keys. The night before I'd dreamed of the translucent Chrystal River, migrating manatees nudging my canoe, fertile grass flats, the cold bubbling springhead. I sat at the counter with my map of Citrus County tracing Highway 44 to 19, Ocala to Dunnellon. Right before lunch, I went up to Stan's office to ask for Thursday and Friday off, but the look on his face said he was the one wanting to talk to me.

"Something going on around here I need to know about?"

"No, sir."

"I don't like folks causing trouble."

His office had a single window, a view of the garbage dumpster, the Dollar General. "I know you don't."

"Just remember, you hear?"

"I sure will."

He shuffled papers, shifted a computer mouse in the shape of a baseball. "So, what'd you come up here to talk about?"

I'd have to settle on a day trip to the springs and that was never enough. Goddamn you, Darcy. "Nothing," I said, "It was nothing."

AT THE COUNTER, I STARED AT THE MAP'S squiggly lines. All this had me thinking about my own mother, something I didn't like to dwell on. Like Darcy, she'd been a teenager when she had me, left me with her elderly folks in Atmore, Alabama. It wasn't a bad life. They did their best, but I knew from my grandparents' whispers my mother never amounted to a thing. Without me, she'd failed in this world, and I couldn't help but wonder if she'd kept me with her, maybe we'd have succeeded. Oh, hell who was I fooling? Maybe things would have turned out worse. Look at Darcy and Will.

With a yellow highlighter, I routed an overnighter to Crystal River with stops at my favorite springs along the way, Ginnie Springs, Blue Springs, Poe Springs. Mrs. Serency, a woman I'd known for years, came in clutching her keys, wheezing. Finally she caught her breath, explained the brakes on her Oldsmobile tried to kill her.

"I like to run off the road," she said.

I gave her coffee from the machine, helped her to a chair. "Well, you're here. We'll take care of things."

Mrs. Serency's younger son arrived to take her home. Her keys were still sitting on the counter when Darcy opened the door. I was so irritated she'd returned, I said, "See that Olds? It's all yours, baby." I shoved the keys toward her, went back to my map, circling places I wanted to see—Salt River, Little Coon Gap. I didn't give a crap about the bum brakes. Darcy wouldn't make it past the parking lot before realizing she had a lemon. Let her see where stealing gets you.

"Come this close to losing my goddamn job," I said when I saw she'd not left.

"I don't want a car, Ray. I'm here to say I'm sorry."

I rested the highlighter over Sheephead Creek.

"I want to come to the lake. See you a while. Talk?"

Something about her had softened. Maybe whatever she'd been

doing was done. I folded the map, left it on the shelf under the register. I didn't know what else could be said between us. "I don't think that's a good idea."

"Please?"

IT WAS NEARLY DARK, AND DARCY hadn't arrived. I'd never asked where she was staying. I ate a three-egg omelet, thanks to my neighbor, diced tomatoes, cheddar, Louisiana hot sauce, washed it down with a Busch, ended up like I always do in my chair by the window with another beer, blaming myself about that boy, but this time I stopped. Just then, Jake's dogs, the lakeside alarm system, went crazy.

Darcy stood on the landing, offered a bottle of pinot noir, a fifth of Johnnie Walker.

"We got till Sunday?"

A mention from the old days made me weak at the knees, but I gathered myself. Didn't want her plowing over me again. "Leaves plenty of time for you to explain."

"Been a long time," she said, surveying the room. "You been wondering where I've been?"

I nodded, thought I'd play along till she opened up. Depending on how long it took, that is. I poured Johnnie Walker. When it was in front of me, I couldn't resist. I handed her a tumbler. "Clean out of wine glasses."

That made her smile.

"So where *have* you been?"

She sipped wine so long I didn't think she'd answer. "Spent some time with my mother," she said, and tipped her cup to me. "Big mistake. What about you? Keeping busy?"

"Call it that."

"No special lady?"

There weren't beans to talk about in that department, and I wasn't ready to reveal one iota about myself. I worried Jake might stop by, and I'd have to explain Darcy's visit, so I turned off the porch light.

"Listen. Never have been one for small talk," I said. "That was lots to ask of me, taking them cars."

"The boss never did know. Did he?"

"*Darcy.*"

She poured another drink, sat in my chair. "Strange to see all the lights on the place. Looks different. Like it's not at all where I used to live."

I let her take in the house a while, then I said, "I need to know what it is you're doing."

Darcy reached in her back pocket for a list, unfolded it. I counted five scribbled names I didn't know, handed it back.

"One by one," she said. "Stealing the pants off 'em. Hunting all the dealers down. Get me my purse."

"Shit," I said, as she unzipped the bag. I touched the cash. Must have been thousands.

"Nobody can find me using Stan's cars. I'm getting off scot free. You want in?"

The look in her eyes was like the time she came from across the lake during the tropical storm, eager and playful. I had to turn away.

She went on, tapping her chin. "Just one thing. I need to figure out what to do with this guy up in Jacksonville. He's behind it all."

"Darcy, stop. You got to forget. You can't—"

"Bring Will back?" Her voice was shaky. She finished her drink, set the tumbler down on the coffee table. "Why'd you give him money? Why?"

"Goddamn it, Darcy," I said, taking her arm, yelling louder than I meant, "I tried. You started too late is what. It was too damn late."

She cried, so I poured another whiskey. All I could see was my own mother, calling out at me and grandpa from the front seat of that pickup, windows down, wind tangling her long hair. If she hadn't wanted me, what was there for me to do about it? Not a goddamn thing. You can't make a mother want you, can you?

"It's not *my* fault," she said, wiping her face. "Is it?"

I couldn't stand the sobbing, so I got my jacket meaning to leave, hoping she'd be gone when I returned in an hour or so, but she got up, came across the room for me.

"Is it, Ray?" she asked again, and though I was mad, I didn't have the heart to tell her it *was* her fault, but the look on her face as she took my chin in her hands said she knew. I was off guard I guess is the only way to explain it, and when she put her arms around me, I caved. It was like all this time she'd been gone there was a sinkhole under my nose waiting for me to collapse in it.

Darcy brought the whiskey to bed with us, pulled the curtains to let moonlight in, and in that light I saw how frail she'd become. I ran my hands along her collarbone, ribs.

"Skin and bones," I said.

Around 1 a.m., I woke to her staring at me, fingers combing my hair. I knew I had to confess.

"That last time Will came to me?"

"Shhh," she said, putting her finger to my lips.

"No. It's important." I pulled her close, steadied myself. "I gave him money to tide him over. Because, I *knew*. I knew that feeling, Darce. It was the reason I got all messed up with drugs."

She sat up, pulled her knees to her chest.

"My own mother left me. It was my grandparents that raised me."

"You never told me that. Did you tell Will?"

"Wish I had."

She played with the sheet, twisting it, pulling it straight. I was afraid she'd start to sob again, but I was ready for it.

"Look," I said. "I don't blame her. I don't blame you." I waited, and when I saw she wasn't going to cry, I said, "I went looking for her one time. My mother."

She ran her hand along my chest, then stopped. "You find her?"

I nodded.

"What'd she say?"

"She didn't know who I was."

Darcy leaned in to me again, and I waited for more questions, but eventually she was breathing soundly, and I thought we'd come to an understanding, a place I'd wanted all along. I'd sleep a happy man. Later, I felt Darcy get up, imagined her sitting in my chair contemplating light skipping the lake. I wondered how hard it would be for her, but then I figured we'd make it soon enough. Over the lake a barred owl called *who-cooks-for-you* clear as a bell, a sign this was a night that would not keep secrets. It called again and before the mate answered, I was asleep.

IN PUTNAM COUNTY THERE ARE 264 LAKES covering nearly 50,000 acres, at least a dozen of them so-called twin lakes with lean connecting land masses. There's a set of twins behind Lake Nelle, small kidney-shaped ones called north and south twins, junior lakes, or up and down lakes, the larger of the two with no cabins on it at all, and the southernmost one inhabited by an old-timer named Leland Sikes. Once Jake and I went over there to buy a floating dock. Aluminum sheds and home-made plywood lean-tos were scattered about the property. Resurrection ferns rooted in the gutters of his cabin, commandeered the entire sagging roof. He'd taken to living in a travel trailer.

Before things went bad, when Darcy still lived here, we woke one Saturday morning to explosions coming from the twins. Gunshot or fireworks we couldn't tell. We followed the smoke and racket through loblollies and live oaks to discover Leland's sheds and house in flames. He stood shoulder deep in the lake, hollering. Darcy and I rolled the house trailer out of harm's way, dodging the blaze. Turns out he'd saved gallons of gasoline waiting on the world to end. By accident, he'd taken a rifle to a squirrel, shot a five-gallon gas container instead.

Darcy told him, "Well, Leland, you just about brought Florida to a close on your own."

That morning after Darcy came to me, I woke to what sounded like hammering explosions from that time at Leland's house. Before I opened my eyes, I sniffed for smoke, tasted a long night of whiskey fire on my tongue. Eyes still closed, I felt for Darcy, came up with wadded sheets. She was gone.

"Ray!" I could make out Stan's voice, the sound of knocking not bullets. I found my jeans, opened the door.

Stan took one look at me, said, "You promised nothing was going on. You promised me, Ray." He took a lump of keys from his pocket. "These yours?"

I studied them one by one. "They are. What're you doing with them? Where were they?"

"At the shop. You got an extra set?"

"Not altogether like that."

I went to the drawer by the sink, rummaged about, held up my extra shop and house keys, found the truck key under foil ketchup packets. "I don't understand."

"That woman come looking for you? She must have stole your set—" He looked around the room at the empty wine bottle on the floor. "Right out of your damn pocket. Let herself in my shop."

"She take my truck?" I opened the door. There was my Dodge, but the Taurus was gone.

"Taurus is in the parking lot at the shop."

The wind was picking up, brushing circles across the glassy lake. The windows in Darcy's cottage sparkled, winked. "I can't make sense of this."

"*Ray*," Stan said, taking my shoulder. "She took the Oldsmobile. The one with the bad brakes."

THE PUTNAM COUNTY SHERIFF'S OFFICE told Stan the car was at Deep Creek in Hastings. He preached all the way from Hawthorne about how he'd built Stan's Auto from scratch, how I better not blunder it. When we got to Palatka, I began to piece it together.

"She was on her way to Jacksonville," I said, interrupting Stan's rant. We were at the crest of Memorial Bridge. Funny how the St. Johns River looked blue from up there, not at all like the brown tea water it really was. "They'll trace her back to me I'm sure."

"Let's see how it pans out. See what they ask first. Don't volunteer nothing."

"But I didn't do anything. Just let her borrow keys," I said, thinking of all that cash in her purse. "I'll tell the law the truth so it doesn't look like I'm hiding nothing."

"Don't you tell them a thing till I talk to 'em first."

"But what's the matter—"

"Do you want your job?"

"Yes, sir."

"Well, then let me do the talking. I don't want any unnecessary attention on Stan's Auto. You hear me?"

Stan's hands trembled against the steering wheel.

For ages, I'd been wallowing so in my own despair I'd hardly noticed if Stan had troubles himself. He seemed as honest as they come, stern and pious, but honest. I needed to come to terms with the fact my judgment was rotten. Just past Hastings, Stan slowed, made a right, eased down to the boat ramp. Wild mallow grew six feet tall in the ditches. Tree frogs barked and clacked. Stan opened the door, immediately fighting gnats, stood on tiptoes toward the wreck, winced at the sight.

"Jesus," he said, covering his eyes. "Mrs. Serency is going to kill me. Listen, don't come down till I signal you."

I started out of the truck. "Stan? What's going on? Something I ought to know about?"

He leaned in, his eyes mean as hell. "We'll forget you said that. Get back in. I'll call for you like I said."

I sat in the truck unable to move, just like the night Darcy and I found Will's car smashed against a pine tree on Old Hawthorne Road. I'd hoped telling her the truth would give Darcy freedom. Maybe it only gave her more incentive to punish people. I shut my eyes. All I could see was her face against mine.

I rolled the window down. The tannic creek smelled of sweet mud and cypress. There was more to the story of my mother. I found her in Evergreen, Alabama, near I-65, the most desolate town I'd ever seen. She was working at Bedsole's Five and Dime, and for fifteen minutes on an April morning, I milled around the store, watching her shelve chocolate Easter rabbits, caramel-filled eggs in pink and yellow foil. Finally, I got the nerve to stand in front of her.

"Hi," I said.

"Can I help you?" she said, this cocky sultriness coming off her like fumes. It had been nine years, but I hoped she'd recognize me like it was a day. "Well? What do you need? Are you deaf?"

I was hurt and angry, reached across, grabbed a chocolate bunny. I waited outside on the sidewalk, heart racing, hoping she'd try to stop me, call me a thief, but she went about her business. I often wonder if she ever realized it was me, or what would have happened if I'd simply told her who I was, maybe even talked to her a while, forgiven her. Opening the car door, looking down toward the crowd forming at the Oldsmobile, I thought, that's what I should have told Will. Forgive her, goddamn it. Forgive her before it's too late.

Paramedics directed a tow truck down the embankment. Stan

checked over his shoulder at me as he talked to the sheriff. I knew whatever it was Darcy did would haunt me sooner or later, but at least when I watched the lake at night from my chair by the window, I wouldn't wonder if she'd return. I'd blame myself for something else. Stan waved for me, so I started toward him. For the first time in years, I wondered where my mother might be because I knew what it was I needed to tell her.

Grounded

THE CROP DUSTER WAS NAMED FOR his mother's ornery great uncle, Hawthorne Eustis Middleton. Young Hawthorne never took to it. When he was twenty-years-old, his hometown of Deep Creek, Florida, was stunned by a summer of hurricanes. Potato fields were waterlogged, the St. Johns River flooded, livestock went missing, and roads were blocked. As Hawthorne accessed damage from his father's Cessna Ag-Cat, he spied Jimmie Solano's prize Black Angus stranded on an overturned bass boat.

"My God. You're a hawk," Jimmie said.

That name stuck.

Years later, on a sunny afternoon in April, the Hawk nursed a cup of coffee at Johnny's Diner like a bird of prey with his wings clipped. For weeks he'd suffered from a mystery illness—dagger toothaches and swinging vertigo. Dr. Seymour extracted an infected molar, and prescribed pain killers. He cautioned of abscesses gone septic and sudden blindness, and suggested a month on the ground to heal.

Ordinarily this time of year, Hawk dusted from daybreak to dark. From his perch at the lunch counter, he studied the clear sky. In the Ag-cat, the river would be a sepia mirror, the plane's reflection skating loops and knots. A fellow named Abernathy from South Georgia was hired to take his place. Earlier, Hawk watched his replacement's halted, unskilled moves in disgust.

Hawk fidgeted. Maybe later if he was feeling better, he'd drive out to the hangar, sit in the cockpit, and listen to some Credence

Clearwater Revival. He checked the clock; his wife was late. He pictured Kiki dawdling at the gas station, ripping the gold cellophane from a pack of Marlboro Lights, flashing those dark blue nails of hers. She'd be bitching about their marriage to the handsome cashier. A needling sensation in Hawk's right molar flared, and he massaged his jaw as if that would somehow help.

Behind him, potato farmers huddled over fried chicken specials—a thigh and a leg, mashed potatoes and cornbread muffins. The thought of food was nauseating, but it was their talk that made him sicker. They wouldn't shut up about the new developer in town like he was a god come to save them. Deluca this, Deluca that. It was sacrilegious to sell generations-old farmland. Otherwise, North Florida would end up like South Florida, all highways and cookie-cutter subdivisions.

"Take your pick. Golf course, condos, shopping centers," Johnny called from the pickup window. It was as if he'd taken to parceling out real estate instead of burgers.

"Don't matter to me." Hawk recognized the raspy voice of Beck Tocoi, an old buddy of his father's. Beck's fifteen-hundred acres sidled up to the St. Johns River. "Long as they pay me my due."

Baker Wells was in on the jokes, too. Not one of the men seemed the least bit ashamed of themselves. A pot of coffee was on. Soon, they'd move on to key lime pie. His stomach roiled.

"What you going to do, Johnny? Golfers don't eat mashed taters and gravy." Old man Taylor had gone up to the window with his empty plate. His land, slap dab in the center of Deep Creek, would be a prime spot for the welcome center, community pool and clubhouse. Hawk wondered if he was thinking that, too.

Johnny mopped his brow with a greasy towel. He winked at Hawk. "Whatever they want I'll fix it."

"You'll need a liquor license," Taylor hollered. "Craft beers and fancy labels. Spud Lite. Gold Tader IPA."

Beck stood, and hitched his pants. He cleared his throat, and paused. "I present you, Cabbage Swamp Ale."

They hollered, and slapped their knees. Somebody drummed a tabletop. Hawk searched his pockets for an ibuprofen, chased it with lukewarm coffee. He pushed his chair in; it screeched against the tile. "I can't listen to another minute of this." He didn't realize he'd spoken out loud, proof medicine can talk. All eyes were on him.

"Hawk, my man. Don't you want in?" Johnny said. "Gonna make a damn killing."

"You know I don't own property. I'm a crop duster."

A voice from the back of the diner said, "More like a sourpuss to me."

Hawk looked to see who it was. A coy-looking man he didn't recognize grinned.

"You can fly the rich folk in from wherever it is they're coming," Johnny said.

"Colorado," Taylor said, leaning back, crossing his legs. "New York City."

Hawk made a face. That would be like driving a sky bus. "So help me God—"

"You're looking green around the gills," Taylor said. "Why don't you sit down?"

Johnny handed Hawk a menu. "You been here going on an hour, and all you had is coffee. Let me fix you something to eat."

Taylor leaned over to Johnny. "He's waiting on Kiki."

Somebody snickered, and Hawk knew what they were thinking, that she was running around on him again. His face went red. "She's late is all."

"Ask her boss where she is," Beck said. "Here he comes."

Kiki had ditched waiting tables at Johnny's for selling real estate for Deluca. Hawk had never met the man. He'd pictured a bald head and wire-rimmed glasses, and he was right, but there was also a goatee and a bowtie, and a hell of a lot of confidence. Deluca strode in like a movie star. Johnny hurried to greet him, and the men stood up like they were receiving Jesus Christ. Taylor said, "This here is Kiki's husband."

Johnny leaned in, "He's not so fond of your grand scheme."

"Maybe I can change his mind." Deluca extended his arm. "Milo Deluca."

Hawk buried his palms in his jean pockets.

Deluca shrugged. "Pleased to meet you, too."

That got the crowd laughing.

"You need to know," Hawk raised his voice to drown out the

commotion. Grown men acting like silly boys. "You need to know some of us like our town just like it is."

Deluca gazed out the plate-glass window at an avalanche of concrete and overturned grocery carts. Over his shoulder, he said, presumably to Hawk. "You see that there?"

"I see it. Home to crack dealers. Those buildings hadn't seen renters in twenty-five years."

"That's my point," Deluca said. "When we get finished with them, there'll be a waiting list a mile long. Condos, duplexes, lofts."

Hawk picked up his cap off the counter, and headed for the door. He didn't know what a loft was, nor what Deep Creek needed with one. "I can't listen to this."

"At least your wife's on our team."

Hawk stopped dead still. "What did you say?"

"Your wife. She's on the forefront of turning this town around."

Hawk parted the group, and stepped right up to Deluca. He studied the man's bowtie, and fancy dress pants. He looked ridiculous. How on earth did these men in Wrangler jeans and white T-shirts keep a straight face? Hawk wanted to yank his stupid-looking goatee. "Don't bring Kiki into this."

"But, my friend," he said, smiling. "She's already in."

The way he said friend made Hawk's blood boil. "You're not my friend. You're going to ruin this town."

"You'll be better off. I'm giving this place life."

Life my ass, Hawk thought. He wanted Deluca *out* of his life, and *out* of his town. Deluca started to speak again, and Hawk didn't want to hear another word he had to say, so he stepped forward, and shoved. Deluca stumbled, and Taylor caught him.

"What, the hell?" Deluca said.

A pall fell over the room. Hawk's face stung. Johnny shook his head, and left for the kitchen, saloon doors swinging. Hawk scanned the diner for support, but Baker and Beck stared into their coffee. Hawk made for the door, aware of hot eyes on his back. Forks clinked against melamine.

Outside, as he leaned on his truck, he thought what have I done? Baker trotted up the sidewalk calling for him. The sun was hot. He'd forgotten his shades. Hawk squinted.

"Son," Baker said. "We need to talk."

Hawk nodded toward the diner. "About that." He assumed Baker wanted an explanation of the scene he'd just made. "I'm not myself. I've come down with something."

"I heard," Baker said. There was an uncomfortable pause. "Listen—"

"I'll be ready to fly next week. I swear. Be all back to normal."

Baker put his hand on Hawk's shoulder. "Even when you get better, we won't need you this season. We'll put down sod in May. Some folks in Jacksonville paid us outright on the harvest."

"Sod?" Hawk said. "That's not farming. Sod's growing in my Aunt Alma's backyard. What about your chipping contracts?"

Baker looked away. "We never even got one from Frito-Lay."

Hawk rested his hand over his heart like it was about to break.

"Last year contracts came in so low," he said. He turned from Hawk, and set his eyes on something up the street. "We could make more selling twenty-pound bags of sebagoes at the flea market. We've not made a dime more than we did ten years ago. It's a dwindling life."

Hawk rubbed his forehead. The news was hard to process. "It's just wrong."

"Listen," he said. He got that faraway look again. "Before you hear it from somebody else, we're in negotiations with Mr. Deluca."

All Hawk could think about was Baker's grandson. He remembered that little boy at nine-years-old driving a truckload of potatoes to the packing house. He had to stand to shift gears.

"What will Little Baker do?"

"That boy never was a farmer. You and I both know all BJ likes to do is drive tractors."

HAWK WATCHED BAKER GO BACK INSIDE the diner. More than likely the men were having a laugh at his expense. He took deep measured breaths to try to forget what he'd done, and what Baker had said. But, sod? Baker was putting down sod? Farmland was meant for sustenance, for farm to table, for handing down to Baker Junior. All Hawk owned was half an acre, and a clapboard house but when he was in his Ag-cat, Hawk soared like a territorial red tail. It was as if *he* had been the one to cultivate and protect all this land, not the farmers. Hell, Hawk knew Deep Creek better than its landowners. Baker's property was a sprawling beauty with islands of magnolias and live oaks, cabbage with a blue-purple hue. Before potatoes broke the surface, the lean rows were perfectly parallel, a study in geometry. The land was tethered generations deep, washed by torrential summer floods, warmed by unforgiving Florida heat. The sight of it all gave him hope. That's what he should have told Deluca. It made him want to set down his own roots, and raise a family. He couldn't imagine life without the huge expanse of space, and endless patches of green. Hawk inhaled and steadied himself, but the images came despite the effort—beige subdivisions burgeoning from the ground like briers, circular cement driveways lined with sycamore seedlings. Hawk teetered, lost his balance and puked in the azalea bushes.

HAWK SLEPT ON THE SOFA DREAMING he was clinging to a plywood raft in the Atlantic Ocean. Steel-toed boots pulled him below the surface. He waved at Kiki where she posed on the beach painting her nails. The plywood sank. Overhead, silver-backed minnows soared like scale-cloaked birds. Hawk grabbed at clouds that broke into slimy bits. He woke with a start to the sharp odor of nail polish, and the memory of the Wells family farm. Hawk felt like he'd been run over by an eighteen-wheeler.

Kiki watched him with a perturbed expression on her face. It gave him a fright to see her painting her nails just like in the dream. It was another coat of that god-awful blue.

"You had to pick a fight with my boss? Have you lost your mind?"

Hawk closed his eyes at the memory. "I feel sick."

"A toothache's no reason to go bullying people. My God, Deluca's my boss. If he wasn't such a good sport, he'd of fired me."

"You stood me up. It wouldn't have happened if you hadn't stood me up."

She started in on her toes, propping her leg on a chair. "I had to study. My real estate test is coming up. I clean forgot about lunch."

There wasn't a hint of apology in her voice. Hawk braced for another round of nausea. "Can you get me some crackers. A little ginger ale?"

He closed his eyes. The refrigerator door opened. The pantry door slammed.

"Here," she said, handing him a glass and a stack of Saltines.

Hawk eased up against a pillow. "Did you know about Baker Wells?"

She was packing a cooler with a six-pack of Pepsi, a quart of Plant City strawberries, and an angel food cake. "That's old news."

"The doctor says I can't fly for a week. Something about a bad infection."

She inspected a box of microwave popcorn. "There's nothing wrong with you."

"Must be something to it." Hawk felt in his pocket and held up the pill bottle.

"They'll prescribe anything to anybody these days."

"Dr. Seymour doesn't know what's wrong. I don't know what I'm going to do. You don't know how it feels to be stuck down here."

Hawk leaned back, and closed his eyes. The crackers were a mistake. "I wish you wouldn't take the test. I thought you loved Deep Creek," he said, swallowing a pain pill. The ginger ale tasted of sheet metal.

"I do love it. I want to make something of it."

"Deluca walks into town, starts teasing desperate farmers with all this money, and they're hungry."

"It's not teasing. It's real."

"They've all been living hand to mouth for years."

"And you want them to keep on living like that?" Kiki asked.

"It's tradition. It's America. And, if they don't have land to dust, I can't dust. And if I can't dust, then what is it I'm supposed to do for a living?"

"As usual, it's all about you." Kiki started on her toenails. "Farmers are selling off land because it's the end of agriculture in America as we know it. We're going to be eating tomatoes and squash grown in laboratories."

"What in the hell are you talking about?" Her enunciation was different. "Honest to God, I don't think I could pick you out in a crowd."

Kiki poured coffee into a thermos. "I got to pull an all-nighter. There's 40 flashcards on probate law I need to know by Wednesday."

He held up a red coffee tin. "It's in Spanish."

She snatched it. "It's Cuban espresso. That's why."

Hawk glanced at the rug he'd bought at the outlet mall. It matched the blue in the sofa perfectly, just as he'd hoped, but the edges were fraying. He turned to the creamy polish drying on Kiki's nails. This was not the blue of the sky or the Atlantic Ocean. Hawk wondered what name Maybelline gave it. "What in the world kind of blue *is* that?"

Kiki fanned her fingers. "I wish you could be more progressive."

"Progressive?" he couldn't believe Kiki's vocabulary. As newlyweds, Kiki crawled under the Cessna with him, and helped change tires. She'd climbed up on the wing and held torque wrenches and wire strippers. On his thirtieth birthday, she'd stood in his uncle Sam Middleton's field one hot afternoon and flagged him down with a six-pack of icy Michelob and a double order of fried shrimp and Datil pepper squash from O'steen's. "I miss the old Kiki."

"Well, the new Kiki's got to study. This test is going to whoop her ass."

Hawk inspected her overnight bag: *Real Estate for Dummies*, tooth brush, makeup bag. "Where are you going?"

"I told you. To study. My friend Deb is taking the test, too. We're holing up at the office."

He opened the cabinet. "Where's my Maxwell House?"

"I threw that out. It's *pedestrian*."

"I can't understand a word coming out a your mouth these days." Hawk studied the bag of food. It was enough to last a week. "Where are you *really* going?"

She parted her hair, pulled the brush through tangles. "Stop interrogating me. All that's over."

"But—"

"That flame burned itself out a long time ago. I told you all that." The phone rang, and on her way to the front door, Kiki answered it.

He wished she hadn't brought up the past. Like he didn't have enough to worry about. Her fling with the Hess driver had been brief, but almost ended their marriage. He'd forgiven her, but there was always a nagging sensation she wasn't telling the truth. Hawk turned over the bottle of nail polish to see the name. *Storm Surge*. Well, if that wasn't appropriate.

"Sure, he's here. Hold on." Kiki handed Hawk the receiver.

"Wait. Don't go yet," he said.

"Hello?" the receptionist said. "Mr. Hawthorne?"

"It's me."

"Dr. Seymour wants you to come in. He's found something."

Kiki admired her storm-surged nails, while Hawk listened to the receptionist go on about his x-rays. He tried to imagine a mother's silhouette, shifting babies from hip to hip, but it wouldn't come. She pointed at her watch, and gathered her bags.

Kiki was closing the Volkswagen door when Hawk got out to the driveway in his sock feet. "My teeth. The dentist has something to tell me. I think it's bad news."

"Oh, for heaven's sake. There's nothing wrong with your teeth. Stop being a hypochondriac."

He leaned in through the car window. "I've got headaches to beat the band. I can't hold down food. What if I can't fly again?" Hawk clutched her arm. "Ever?"

Kiki jabbed the key in the starter. "You're exaggerating."

"Don't go," he said. "Please?"

"For God's sake," Kiki said. She looked at him, and immediately her face changed.

"Damn, honey. You look awful." She touched his jaw. "You're blue." She made a face. "Like all the life's gone out of you. Go on to the dentist. Everything will straighten itself out."

Hawk detected a hint of kindness in her voice, or maybe it was pity. Either one was a long time in coming. "I love you, Kiki," he said, and jumped back as she gunned the engine.

THE CEILING SPUN AT DR. SEYMOUR'S OFFICE.

"Sometimes when toxins soak into the body," the dentist was saying. "They travel through the roots of your teeth."

Hawk closed his eyes, and saw bulldozers uprooting, and enormous signs with orange letters: *Owner Financing. Will Divide.* He heard buzzing chain saws, and imagined watching all this destruction at eye level.

"And, then they think they've found an exit," Dr. Seymour said. "But *actually*, they're trapped and stuck to rot out their life inside the tooth. Or, worse."

Hawk touched his chin. "Worse? How could it get any worse?"

The dentist set his hand on Hawk's shoulder. "Tell me this. Your father was a crop-duster, too?"

"All his life. He was a Green Beret. I started as his loader back in '78. What's this got to do with anything?"

Dr. Seymour rolled away toward his desk, legs in the air like a joy ride. "Was he ever ill?"

Hawk's father, Ben, died in his fifties. "They said it was natural causes."

Dr. Seymour flipped through papers, his back to Hawk. "Do you use gloves and masks when you load the plane?"

"Sometimes—"

The dentist rolled around to face him, his lips pinched. "Hawthorne, I'm worried. There's a specialist in Jacksonville."

The room twirled. "Am I going to die?"

"Don't get ahead of yourself. There's treatment—"

Hawk held on to the chair, and shut his eyes again. "Do you know what it's like to be up there in the sky?"

"I've been on my share of airplanes—"

"To be up there. Really up there. The plane's talking to you, the clouds are talking to you."

"There's something called chelation therapy," the dentist said. "It's for extreme chemical buildup—"

"My mama would park the car at the roadside, and we'd watch Daddy dust. He'd be going 130 miles a hour, inches above the potatoes, and then zoom up over the powerlines, beautiful as ballet. I belong up there, doc. I really do."

Dr. Seymour handed a note to the nurse. She left the room, and the dentist folded his hands under his chin. "Have you considered going on disability?"

Hawk jumped out of the chair. The tool tray toppled as he wrestled the paper bib from his neck. "I'm fine. It's a toothache. Kiki said so. It's a damn toothache."

"Wait," the dentist said. "You can't leave."

The nurse ran after Hawk. On the street, she called to him, her voice high-pitched and desperate.

THE HANGAR WAS NOTHING MORE THAN an aluminum shed in the field behind Leroy Seaton's house. Hawk yanked the doors open; it was as if he'd been gone a year. The barrels, with their skull and crossbones labels, lined the back wall. He wondered if there was truth to Dr. Seymour's theory. He slid his palm across the shiny propeller, and the plane's red body, and climbed into the cockpit. Disability? That would be the death of me, Hawk thought, not my teeth. Hawk lingered, taking in the smell of the soil. He'd flown with Jack and Coke hangovers alongside blue forks of lightning, and once, before a tropical depression drowned acres of potatoes, he'd ascended Deep Creek in a muffled pre-storm calm. When he'd landed, that little corner of Florida seemed less complicated, as if he'd been privy to a secret. If he could handle the mechanics of a violent sky, he was equipped for turmoil handed to him on land, along with a dozen toothaches. He started the engine, and a deep thrum pulsed through the sole of his boots. Hawk would not be grounded.

THE PLANE BUCKED ALONG THE MAKESHIFT runway. On takeoff, Hawk was comforted at the sight of drooping clapboard houses and doublewides, pickup trucks zigzag on lawns. At the St. Johns River, he throttled down, flew low over splintered docks, the familiar bend thick with eel weed and alligator lilies where years ago from his dad's jon boat, they'd fished for channel cats and flatheads. At a stand of weeping cedars, he banked right, backtracked inland, grazing the muddy snake of the river until ripples peeled the tannic surface. He dipped over Cabbage Swamp Road, and followed a gaggle of gravel lanes. Gaining altitude, he looped toward Floyd Packers, and then, Baker's land, already plowed under, and ready for sod.

Somewhere over Beck's property, a crewelwork of new potatoes, Hawk hit a stubborn headwind. His stomach heaved with the turbulence, and Hawk tasted bile. The plane teetered, and he overcompensated. The tail sagged, the plane dropped and plunged, landed sideways, right wing hooking soil, propeller churning potato plants like a combine. His head knocked the windshield; he swallowed blood. Pain lit deep. Unable to differentiate new aches from old, he leaned forward, and started the engine. It groaned. Wisps of smoke drew from the hood. He eased open the door.

The engine hissed, and Hawk smelled smoke. He climbed down from the plane, and crawled toward uprooted potato plants, tiny white flowers burgeoning from dark green leaves. They must be saved. With his good hand, he shoveled a shallow trench, and gathered the back-flung plants. He tucked them into the hole so their tendrils would root, fusing just below the surface, and further to the karst caves of the aquifer, outliving them all.

Pickup trucks gathered at the road. Farmers in coveralls circled, clenching John Deere caps. Their faces blurred; their familiar voices were amused:

"He's grasping at straws if he thinks those plants will take."

"Never did think he was right in the head."

"We should a seen this coming."

The Ag-cat's engine flamed. Men hollered. Paramedics tromped through pocked soil. Fire extinguishers frothed milky clouds. Gloved hands were on Hawk's shoulders and legs. Suspended on a stretcher, hovering over shifting land, the blue sky was above him. Hawk opened his arms wide as wings.

Alligator

AFTER THE HURRICANE, DEAN SLEPT during the day in a hammock on the second-floor porch to protect his home from storm-looters. At night, from the balcony, he dumped sulfur water on the heads of thieves. Seven days in, there was still no electricity. Rationed canned corn and kidney beans grew tiresome. Dean caught mangrove snappers off the coquina seawall, grilled them on gas fumes until the tank went dry. From the toxic floodwaters of his garage, he salvaged charcoal briquettes, and sunned them on the cobblestone lanai. The old house, reeking of mildew and wood rot, swelled with humidity.

On the eighth night, a mournful bellow roused Dean. He tracked it down streets of unearthed trees, and spiny debris. At the coquina seawall between the car-dealer's gaudy Victorian mansion and the old Minorcan's bungalow, a bull gator sprawled in the brackish Matanzas River. Bony scutes lined his vibrating spine. The seductive song became a chainsaw gargle of bass notes and clacking cans. It was a hypnotic formula. Water beads danced on the surface. Though man and alligator were separated by a waist-high wall, Dean stepped away. He'd seen his share of tours at the town's alligator zoo. This was a mating performance or territorial display, either one a fight to death. Floridians know the stories. Alligators make unlikely homes of golf-course ponds and concrete culverts, but here, in this salty river at the town's center, spitting distance from the Atlantic Ocean, how would this freshwater beast ever survive?

Before the category-four hurricane, St. Augustine had been the stuff of glossy brochures—tidy mansions once home to sea captains and railroad tycoons, water oaks garnished with Spanish moss. Then, the sea rose. White caps battered the masonry fort that centuries ago guarded against British raids and shameless pirates. Dislodged docks and barnacled pilings floated ashore. Sailboat masts lodged on ruined lawns like flags to uncharted territory. Now, the historic city was a sinking city of five-foot water marks and drowned cats.

Dean's own house was a mess. Floorboards buckled. Plaster walls blossomed with mold. The back porch disconnected from the foundation; his Toyota Prius drifted two blocks to the Huguenot Cemetery. The storm stole the landscape, too. The once delicious odor of a briny low-tide—oyster beds teaming with flower anemones, fiddler crabs denning below tidal sands—was now fetid with death. Bloated Redfish and American toads rotted in bubbling algae. Yet, long before the storm, Dean was unmoored. Recently widowed, his wife of 22 years dead in her sleep, he understood solitude's cruelty. Here, beneath salt-burned mangroves, he'd found a kindred spirit.

THE NEXT EVENING AT SUNSET, THE alligator was gone. Dean looked out to Bird Island, the narrow sand bar between the sea wall and the inlet, where on weekends, boaters anchored, and drank beer. The golden plumes of sea oats, the island's tolerant garrisons, swayed with the breeze, their deep roots fastening the land in place. Perhaps the alligator was hunting for piping plovers among the dunes, but, more than likely, he was gone for good. Dean felt an inexplicable sadness at the creature's absence; he had no business making friends with an alligator. A shrimp boat tacked in the channel raised its trawl nets like an anhinga's wings outstretched to dry. Off to the east, the Bridge of Lions hoisted its leaves for a passing barge. Channel lights winked a green eye, as if giving the go-ahead, the universe making way for something ominous or grand. Dean waited, but nothing happened, and twilight fell, and he started for home. In the storm sewer, water sloshed, metal dinged, and something with great girth shifted. One Halloween years ago, Dean watched a rat slip between the sewer slats, a Kit Kat candy bar in its mouth. Dean crouched, and flashed the cell phone light between the grates. Garnet eyes atop a u-shaped snout flared. Dean climbed on the seawall and peeked over the side. The drain's exit pipe to the river was a wide rusty culvert, large enough for an alligator to enter. The deep catch basin was half full from the morning rain.

"Son of a gun," he said. Survival at its most ingenious.

GRADUALLY, ROADS WERE CLEARED, electricity restored, and Dean's neighbors returned home. Church groups assisted the elderly with lawn work. Side by side, Mormons and Presbyterians sang hymns, dragged branches and bagged seagrass. A tow truck delivered Dean's totaled Prius. Throughout town, curbside debris tripled. It would be weeks before trucks made it to his street. Twenty-four hours a day, the county burned brush piles. Occasionally, a whiff of scorched cedar cleansed the air like shaman smudge.

The first Saturday of the month was cemetery day. At 9 a.m., Mrs. Triay appeared at Dean's door with a wagon of cleaning supplies and potted chrysanthemums. She'd been caretaker to her parents, her in-laws, two late husbands, and now their graves. After Sabra's death, Dean's grief was palpable. He'd asked Mrs. Triay if he'd ever survive. How had *she*? My people, she'd reminded. Her people were the Minorcan slaves of General Turnbull, a British landowner in New Smyrna. In 1778, starved and abused, they escaped the indigo plantations, marching north 70 miles to asylum in St. Augustine. Dean didn't have Mrs. Triay's resolute blood. His ancestors were North Alabama slave owners, like Turnbull; grief and violence was entrenched in Dean's blood line. He doubted a valiant recovery.

"No telling what shape those headstones will be in after that storm," she said, showing off bleach bottles and toothbrushes. The deep-set lettering of Sabra's white granite headstone was an unflappable serif font. Mrs. Triay was an exacting cleaner.

Dean could not meet her eyes. "I'm sorry. I can't go."

"Are you sick?"

He wasn't, but the sky was. It was noxious and vile, a putrid shade of lemon. "Yes," he said. "A fever. A headache."

Mrs. Triay studied his eyes with sympathy or suspicion. He'd lied to her, his neighbor, his champion, his old friend. But there was a secret Dean wasn't ready to share. He helped her to the gate. An awkward goodbye blistered the air. The wagon wobbled behind her.

The truth was this: Sabra wasn't at the cemetery. She was at the house. She was in the yard. This morning, she'd watched Dean through the screened door. She tended the campfire he'd abandoned when electricity was restored. Sabra always wore her long wavy hair loose, but now it was plaited in a single, dour braid. Her posture was no longer meek, but determined. She had not yet spoken. Dean crossed the lane, and there she was in the front porch rocker.

DEAN AND SABRA TOOK LONG WALKS. The roadside trash heaps of the town's elite were impressive—waterlogged designer sofas, antique dresser drawers, soggy drywall papered in brocade and fleur-de-lis. Sabra suggested they bring the wheelbarrow and recover what they could. They riled through upended kitchen cabinets, shredded wallpaper and moldy carpets. This was unlike her. She preferred IKEA to antiques. Dean scored a chipped stand-up-paddle board with missing fins. He found bronze drawer pulls and wrought iron light fixtures. She clapped for joy.

In the back yard, they separated useless junk from salvageable junk. Dean revived tables and chairs, soaked cushions in vinegar concoctions to kill mold. He sanded the warped shelves of a bookcase and studied Sabra as she ran her hands over the treasures. She was different now. Her personality was off-kilter and rude. She ignored Dean's questions. She told rambling stories in a strange, high-pitched doll voice. Should he phone her brother, and explain she'd risen from the dead? What would their friends say? He watched as she arranged wingback chairs and end tables around the fire. Could he trust his eyes? It sure resembled Sabra collecting juice-jar bouquets of spider wort and peanut grass. Shouldn't he be grateful for her return?

"Sabra?" he said.

She must have detected the skeptical tone. She would not make eye contact, and admired her purple fingers stained by spider wort.

"Honey?" He did his best to sugarcoat the question. "Is it really you?"

Sabra walked toward the shade of the mulberry tree, and then out the front gate. He didn't see her for two days.

FRANK, THE INSURANCE ADJUSTOR, WAVED a mildew-detecting wand along Dean's kitchen wall. At each shrill beep, the lanky middle-aged man frowned. Ripping the drywall up four feet was crucial, he explained, as was running commercial exhaust fans and 100-pint dehumidifiers to extract moisture. Upstairs, Frank pointed to tea-colored stains on the ceilings.

"Hate to say it," he said. "You'll need a new roof."

Dean studied the sickly constellations and sallow peninsulas. For days, he'd been wandering around in the dark, Sabra humming at his shoulder. He'd paid no attention to what was over his head. Frank compiled lists, and punched numbers into a laptop. He seemed like the kind of guy who could make sense of hard times. Sabra stood in the doorway, blocking the route to the dining room. Dean wondered if Frank could see her.

"Eventually, you'll need a new air conditioner," Frank said. "All that ductwork under the house? It soaked for days in saltwater, among other things."

During the storm, the river spilled over the seawall collecting everything in its path—sewage and gasoline and E. coli—and rose through the floorboards of Dean's house. Even if he received a hefty check from the insurance company as Frank predicted, it would take forever to return the house to normal. Sabra was deep in thought, her expression as grim and exasperated as his. Maybe she didn't approve of the exhaustive to-do list, either. They'd always thought alike. "It's just too much," Dean said.

Frank scanned the room. His eyes were heavy, full of the weight of the world. He seemed to look straight through Sabra. He shook his head in agreement. "Tell me about it."

For a second, Dean considered sharing his secret. He met Frank fifteen years ago when they'd bought this house. Frank wrote the insurance policy. From time to time, Dean saw him at the hardware store, or having lunch at O'Steens. Frank began to talk of residents raising their houses eight feet for the *next* storm. Dean's attention waned. He didn't have the energy to speculate about future storm surge. Suddenly, Sabra wasn't waiting at the door anymore. Where had she gone? This was all so confusing. Since she'd returned, he didn't know whether to be overjoyed or fearful. Frank went on and on about I-beams, hydraulic bottle jacks, and floor joists. In Sabra's calming voice of long ago, not the strange new timbre, he heard his name from the other end of the house.

"Sabra?" Dean answered.

Frank had stopped chattering. "Dean?" he was saying. "Earth to Dean." Frank was kneeling on the floor, tapping the blonde heart of pine. "I said, you sure wouldn't want to lose these floors. Be a real shame."

Dean's face went red. "That's right," he said, slowly processing Frank's concern. "A real shame."

Frank went outside to measure the dislocated back porch. Dean brewed coffee. It was too much, he repeated to himself as he set out cream and sugar. How was he supposed to go on with his life? It was just too much. He was staring into an empty mug when Frank returned.

"How you been doing, Dean?" Frank said.

The question was complicated. "Sabra," was all Dean could utter. Should he speak of her in past or present tense? He nodded to a news clipping on the refrigerator, Sabra at their retirement party hosted by the tax collector's office. "Two weeks before she died."

Frank studied it. "A real beauty. I was so sorry to hear. If you don't mind me asking, did they ever find out the cause?"

Dean put his hand to his chest. "Her heart." This corner of the kitchen was particularly dark, and the shutters hadn't been opened for months. Suddenly feeling choked, he pulled them apart like accordions, and dust motes floated, light bringing attention to months of neglect. His eyes drifted to another photo—Sabra and himself surrounded by county employees. He handed it to Frank. "Quite the party."

Frank's eyes widened. "Is that the sheriff? In *drag*?"

They laughed, but suddenly, Frank sobered, and studied the picture of Sabra. Dean could tell he was a good man, a thoughtful man. "Frank, mind if I ask you something?"

Frank leaned in, willing to be a confidant. Dean sensed he, too, understood demons.

Sabra appeared in the doorway. "No," she mouthed.

Dean looked from Sabra to Frank, and back again. Frank waited.

"About the floors," Dean said. "Tell me what it is I need to do to save the floors."

THAT NIGHT, DEAN AND SABRA SAT in the wingback chairs by a dying fire. They puzzled over maps for clues of the alligator's origins. Sabra traced her finger over inland fresh-water lakes, sinkholes, and man-made retention ponds. She stopped at the dark line of a tidal creek, a tributary to the Matanzas River.

"Aha. Moses Creek," Dean said. The undeveloped creek was known for enormous hornet nests burrowed in muddy bluffs, nesting flocks of white ibis, and roseate spoonbills, and most importantly, massive sunning alligators.

"Home, sweet, home," Sabra said.

It was a moonless night over the outpost of ghost furniture. It was as if a great party were to descend upon them. In the distance, the alligator's deep bellow broke the stillness.

Sabra stepped from the fire for the first time all day, raised her hand to her ear.

"Want to meet the gator?" Dean asked.

At the seawall, Dean pointed the flashlight into a cluster of mangroves. Their aerial roots were wavy stilts arching high over the water like pelican legs, weaving and crisscrossing, somehow filtering the acidic water, allowing the plant to flourish. He shined the flashlight looking for the alligator's flaming eyes.

"Look," he whispered.

A foraging raccoon plucked fiddler crabs from the mud, chewed them like gum; then, a blast from the shadows, and the alligator's jaws stretched into a perfect V. Sabra screamed. The raccoon was gone. The alligator settled beneath the mangroves, a gray tail dangling from its snout.

"Son of a gun," Dean said. "Son of a gun."

Sabra insisted they stay. She directed Dean's flashlight up and down the alligator's dark frame and jawline. "He's lovely," she said, leaning in close to Dean, and they admired him together until a light rain began to fall.

LIKE THE ALLIGATOR, SABRA WOULD come and go. She

insisted on keeping the fire stoked. Some nights she wept beside it, and refused to come inside. Sleepless nights took their toll. Headaches and blurry vision plagued Dean. Though he admittedly wasn't himself, he gradually understood *this* Sabra was nothing like the old one. This one was emboldened. Sometimes he napped in the hammock during the day, dreaming of who she had been—a quiet, content, sweet woman. This Sabra had more time on her hands. She was up to something. Dean couldn't put his finger on what that was. She had an emboldened mischievous drive. He could see it in her crooked grin. One morning, she got that look again, and he asked her carefully. "What is it that you want?"

Lately, she had become sensitive and easily offended. This time, however, she smiled, and closed her hands around his chin. "I want you to believe in me."

Dean was afraid to tell the truth. What if she could read his thoughts? "Well?" she said.

"Of course." He tried to sound sincere. "Of course, I believe."

Dean left Sabra dozing by the fire, and walked across the street. Mrs. Triay was pruning papaya trees. She set her clippers down. Her cheap flip flops yipped as she walked. "You feeling better?" she asked.

The question confused him, and then he remembered his faked illness. "I sure am," he said. "Thanks for asking. How was the cemetery?" He couldn't stop thinking of how Sabra got here. Had she clawed her way out of the ground? Had she wrecked her burial site in the process? He paused and searched for the right question. "Was everything okay?"

Mrs. Triay stepped closer. "Lots of grime. Twigs and so forth. One big limb down," she said. "But I got Timothy to help."

Dean felt a twinge of guilt. "Thank him for me. I'm real sorry I couldn't make it. Listen," he said, waiting for courage. "Have you seen anything *unusual*?"

Mrs. Triay sunk her hands into the pockets of her housecoat, and raised her head toward the water. Dean remembered her elderly parents; they'd seemed to shrink with the years, but not Mrs. Triay. She was strong, always had been. However, the expression on her face said something different. She looked afraid of him.

"Son, what is it you think I might have seen?"

Sabra appeared on the sidewalk, kicking at a rock.

Mrs. Triay followed his gaze toward the street. "Is there something you want to talk about?"

Dean managed a smile. "No, no," he said, walking away. "I'm fine. I better be going."

"Are you staying hydrated? It's god-awful hot."

Dean backed away. "I'm good. I promise."

Sabra held the gate open. "I told you," she said, her voice stern. "*Believe.*"

WORD GOT OUT ABOUT THE ALLIGATOR. Neighbors stopped to take photographs. Some brought their friends. One of the city's more enterprising homeless residents, an ex-con named Tate, charged tourists five dollars a pop to feed him Milk-Bone dog biscuits. Dean found Tate at the seawall one afternoon with a woman and three children. The youngest boy, no more than four-years-old, tossed a treat. When the alligator lunged, the kids cheered.

"Don't do that," Dean said. "He'll associate food with humans. Somebody'll get hurt."

Tate pocketed his money. "Try and stop me."

"I'll call the police."

Tate accused Dean of ruining a very good business. He left, the woman and her reluctant children, following. Lately, Dean had bouts of clarity. They were contrasted, however, with hours when he was so wrung out with headaches he couldn't think straight. But this was a lucid thought. It was time to call wildlife management before someone got hurt. He'd tell them of their theory, that the alligator originated from muddy Moses Creek. He imagined trappers shooting the alligator with a sleeping dart, taping the snout with duct tape, and hauling it into the back of a truck.

Dean climbed onto the seawall, his decision made. "You're going home, buddy."

THE NEXT AFTERNOON, A FLORIDA Fish and Wildlife truck idled at the seawall. Dean greeted the two officers. They wore rubber hip waders and carried crooked poles and rifles. The older one walked with arthritic pain, his knees bowed. The younger one, slight and rail thin, hopped up on the seawall. When the gator ascended, the big man let out a fetching whistle.

The younger one took pictures with his phone. "Eight feet?"

"At *least*," the big man said.

"I'm the one that called," Dean said. "I know where you need to take him." He checked their name badges. The big one was Officer Wilde; the younger man was Officer Andreu.

"Where we need to take him?" Wilde said. He laughed as he made a cutting motion across his throat. "Tomorrow morning this baby's crossing the rainbow bridge."

"But your website. It says nuisance gators will be relocated."

"The little bitty ones," Wilde said. "Three, four footers."

"The alligator farm," Dean said. "They'd take him."

"If we took every gator we captured to that place," Andreu said, in what sounded rehearsed, "They'd have to build an annex named after us."

The officers laughed.

"But, the storm," Dean said. "The storm disoriented him. He was blown here. He didn't mean to come here."

"Didn't *mean* to?" Wilde said, nodding toward the alligator. "Gator boy's got a brain the size of a pea."

Officer Andreu nodded, and grinned. "You're right about one thing. They do get turned around after a bad storm. Mating season's in April. Problem is it's September, and they think it's spring."

Andreu said they'd return in the morning with police barriers and backup. "Just in case, this bad boy gets hard to handle." He pulled up his sleeve.

There was an ugly cut along his arm, crudely bandaged. "There's a female under one a your neighbor's docks. About six or seven houses that direction," he said, nodding north. "She got away from us."

"Maybe you should have let her be," Dean said.

Wilde and Andreu shared a wink and a grin. Wilde crooked his thumb around his gun holster. "Listen. Gators are opportunists. They lurk. They wait. They—"

"Some kid," Andreu interrupted. He paused dramatically. "That what you want?"

Dean remembered the children lobbing Milk-Bones, and the

mother's encouragement. The truck doors creaked open, and Wilde hollered, "Remember, there's no such thing as a nice gator."

They drove away, but Dean couldn't take his eyes off the alligator. The intricate pattern of horned scutes across its back were artwork. Finally, the creature submerged, the pointy pricks of its spine perforating the surface like jewels.

"YOU'VE GOT TO SAVE HIM," Sabra said.

Dean had made the mistake of telling her about the female alligator, how she mauled the officer, and how the men were coming around in the morning to euthanize the bull gator. Sabra was inconsolable. Dean certainly understood feeling connected to an animal, but this didn't make sense. "Why is saving that gator so important, honey?"

She looked at him as if she'd run across the lawn, never to return. He tried to remember their married life. Had she ever acted like this before?

"I feel bad for the gator," he said. "But, believe me, there's nothing I can do. Plus, sounds like the female ran off. Not without a fight, though. She gave that officer a run for his money." He hoped Sabra would laugh, but instead, she stared off at the sky. The setting sun ignited the arrow tips of palm fronds; they stabbed the sky with orange blood. The fire sputtered, and whittled up from the coals. Never in his life had he laid a fire in summer.

"You have to protect him," she said.

"Are you out of your mind?" Dean remembered Officer Wilde's pistol and snare pole. He had neither weapon. "Damn it, Sabra. We're talking about a wild animal. A dangerous wild animal. I could get myself killed."

She sobbed.

"Shh," he said, glancing across the street. Mrs. Triay sat in her carport at night and watched the moon rise over the fort. "Let's go inside. Somebody might hear you."

She went to the tattered wingback, propped her feet on the ottoman. "I want to sit by the fire."

"My God, Sabra. It's a hundred degrees, if not a thousand."

"Don't yell." She shivered, her teeth chattering.

Dean kindled the fire with palm fronds. Flames shot shoulder-high. He hadn't raised his voice to Sabra, but there was no sense arguing. His face and neck pimpled with perspiration. He was woozy from the heat. Still, Sabra shivered. "Maybe you have the flu?"

She leaned in toward the flames and warmed her palms. "The officers. They're coming tomorrow. *Do* something."

Dean stabbed the palm fronds with the fire iron. The heat was miserable; his head was killing him. "Damn it, Sabra. It's an eight-foot bull gator." He started for the house. "I need a cold beer."

"You never would help me," she said.

At the sweetgum tree, Dean stopped. The venom in her voice was shocking. "What did you say?"

"All those years. You never helped me with a thing."

"Never helped you? I did whatever it was you wanted. I hardly did a damn thing for myself. I waited on you, hand and foot."

Sabra stood slowly. The plush velvet chair formed a garish Victorian backdrop. Her face was rosy, color finally returning to her cheeks. The fire had done her good. Dean refused to let up. "Why are you doing this to me? I've been alone for months. I was taking care of things just fine."

Sabra laughed. "No, you weren't. Look at yourself."

He touched his beard. He'd been wearing the same jeans and T-shirt for days. His eyes were surely crazy, but no more than hers. "I've tried. My God, I've tried. It's nearly killed me. Then, there was the storm, and it was like you died all over again."

She walked toward the front gate. "I didn't leave on purpose."

"Oh, stop with the crying. Those tears aren't real. None of this is real."

"It is real. *I'm* real."

"If it's so real, why can't I tell people about you? Why can't I show you off?"

She stood on one side of the fence, Dean on the other.

"Why? Why, Sabra?"

She didn't answer. She was crying again, and shaking her head. He watched as she ran toward San Marco Avenue. Her words stung. *Had* he neglected her? Had he been a jerk all those years? He ran after, but Sabra crossed the street and disappeared into the maze of St. George Street shops.

"Sabra," he screamed. He stood in the road. Cars swerved and honked.

"Get out of the road. You want to get killed?" A man yelled from his truck.

DEAN STUMBLED TO THE CURB, AND walked home. Mrs. Triay's porch light switched on. She waited at the end of the driveway clutching her housecoat. "I heard a commotion. Are you sure you're okay?"

He snapped. "I'm fine. You hear? I'm fine."

He walked on to the house. At the front door, he turned back. Mrs. Triay was still there at the street, waiting.

DEAN WAS HALFWAY THROUGH A SIX-PACK. He hoped the roaring fire would lure Sabra home. Magnolia leaves crackled. The waxy leaves, fallen from the guarding tree last winter, were a carpet of dry kindling, a natural burglar alarm. Someone was approaching.

"Sabra?" Dean said.

The lean profile of Timothy Triay stepped into the firelight. Timothy was built like his mother, trim and short. His roofing company kept him fit, his arms and face mahogany. Timothy stood, hands in his pockets. Dean wondered what it was like to view the world from rooftops. An omniscient perspective probably kept a man decent. Dean opened a fourth can. He should offer Timothy one, but didn't want him staying long enough to finish it.

"Dean, my mama's concerned about you."

Dean swilled his beer. "Your mother's a sweet lady."

Timothy tossed a magnolia cone into the fire. It had been chewed to death by a squirrel, and would take forever to catch and burn.

"I hate to say it," Timothy said. "You're not well, buddy. I mean, you're just not yourself."

Dean considered that. He'd not been himself since the day Sabra died. Now that she was back, or, was she? He still didn't feel right, but he wouldn't admit it to Timothy. Instead, he tried to give a normal look, and in a calm voice, said, "You tell Mrs. Triay I appreciate her checking on me. Tell her I said goodnight." He gathered his beer, and went inside.

Dean woke to moonlight pressing his eyelids. Memories drew slowly: Sabra running, Timothy's declaration: *You aren't well.* Dean crouched at the side of the bed, his thoughts cottony. The clock read 3 a.m. He'd been an idiot. Mrs. Triay only wanted to help, and he needed it. The secret was destroying him. At sunup, he'd bring strong coffee and the newspaper; he'd explain everything. He'd tell her the truth about Sabra.

Downstairs, the front door opened. Footsteps danced across the hall.

"Dean?" It was Sabra, her voice full of cheer, the softer, kinder version he remembered years ago. It floated upstairs and lingered at the landing. From his bedroom at the top of the stairs, he hesitated.

"Forgive me?" she said. "I shouldn't have said those things."

Dean thought of Mrs. Triay, and his planned confession, but dressed anyway, and took the stairs with care, stopping on the landing. Oyster-shell light fell across the bannister, and poured over Sabra. She had never been more beautiful.

"I didn't know you were so unhappy," he said. "*Before.*"

She offered her arm. "I have something to show you," she said.

"This is real," he said, and then once more to convince himself. "It is."

She nodded, and smiled. "Let's hurry."

They walked outside, arm in arm.

MOONLIGHT AND SHADOWS LACED THE LAWN. Dean assumed she wanted to bask in this dreamy spectacle with him. Then, he spied the upheaval. The wingback chair had been loaded onto the wheelbarrow, warped plywood balanced on top. Sabra tugged at the ottoman. "Give me a hand?"

"What're you doing?"

"Follow me," she said, starting off across the lawn, wheelbarrow bucking.

Dean's broken paddle board teetered like a lever. It took them both to steady the contraption. "We look like old drunks."

She shoved on toward the seawall. Dean assumed they were returning the resuscitated furniture to its prospective roadside heaps. Sabra turned the wheelbarrow on its side. Furniture toppled. She stepped up on the wall like she owned it. "A wide barrier," she said, her arm moving like a conductor's. "You'll build it with all this, and when that gator returns, he won't be able to pass through. He'll be confused, and leave." She snapped her fingers. "Just like that. When the officers arrive, there won't be anything for them to catch."

Dean stepped up on the wall alongside her. The officer had said they were easily confused after storms. After all, that's how the alligator ended up here to begin with. Dean didn't have his flashlight. He squinted toward the mangroves, and thought of Officer Andreu's injured arm. "He may still be here."

"He's hunting," she said. Her certainty surprised him.

"How do you know?"

"I saw him," she said, as if he had the audacity to question her. "Now, what do you think about my plan?"

It was ridiculous, but he was afraid to tell her. "It's pretty ambitious, honey. You think it'll work?"

"Of course, it will."

Her glare was penetrating. Dean knew to tread carefully.

"A barricade is what we need," she went on. "You have chicken wire and wooden stakes from the old vegetable garden."

Dean recalled there were six bundles. "I don't know if I have enough."

"We're only talking about twenty feet or so," she said. "If the fence is four feet high, it'll keep the gator away."

Dean was impressed at her calculations. Years ago, at St. Augustine Beach, Dean watched a group of marine biologists wrangle an injured dolphin. They held fence posts attached to plastic fencing and eventually corralled the dolphin, and whisked him away for surgery. Maybe this wasn't as crazy as he thought. "You know what. We just might be able to do this. And, then, that gator could go wherever he was before all this."

"Like on the map," she said.

Together, they chimed, "Moses Creek."

"Son of a gun." Dean lifted his palm in the air. Oh, how he wanted this to work. For her, for them. Sabra met his hand with a high-five. "You're so smart," he said. "You always were."

"Son of a gun," Sabra said. "I always loved it when you said that."

He spoke slowly, "Son of a gun."

Sabra beamed.

IT TOOK THREE TRIPS TO TRANSPORT the rubble. After a while, they took a break, resting on the wall. Dean said, "That first night? It was like the gator was calling me. Like—" He searched for the perfect word. "A summons."

Sabra kissed his cheek. He'd wanted to bargain. The gesture gave him courage. "I'll do this for you, but I need you to tell me something."

Sabra went quiet. "What?"

He took her slender hands in his. Earlier, they'd been cold, but now they were warm. On cue, his own palms went icy. "All this time. Where've you been?"

"Right here with you," she said in the doll voice. She stepped away, turning a pirouette along the seawall. Dean never knew her to be so graceful. Then, she jumped down, and clapped her hands. "Now, let's get to work."

Dean studied the mangrove roots. "It's a rising tide. We'll have to work fast."

He tossed a nickel, and it dimpled the calm water. No boney scutes or gleaming eyes rose to the mirror surface. Dean peered through the storm sewer slats. "No sign of him here, either." He turned to Sabra. "Guess he *is* out hunting."

Sabra gave him an I-told-you-so smirk. Together, they secured warped plywood sheets at the mouth of the sewer.

"That ought to keep him from getting in," Dean said.

For the next hour, they lifted furniture over the seawall. The only way this would work, Dean thought, is if they arranged the barrier just beyond the mangroves where the water was three-feet deep. The wingback was cumbersome, and made a huge splash. Droplets sprayed Sabra's face. She laughed like a child. Using the paddleboard, Dean ferried the lighter pieces—a wicker table and plywood, and set them on top of the drowned wingback, a cedar trunk and three bookshelves. It was a gangly rag-tag fence line. The paddleboard's foam top took on water; it lilted to the side. Dean was soaking wet, his jeans clinging. Goose pimples traveled down his arms. Sitting around the fire sounded good for a change. In the back of his mind was a needling thought. If Sabra had been here all this time, why hadn't he seen her? There had to be a logical answer. He glanced over at her, and she smiled knowingly, but sternly, as if to say, get back to work.

Dean knitted stakes through chicken wire until another makeshift fence emerged to contain the unwieldy wall. He walked up to his waist in the water to get a better handle on the structure, all the while thinking of the alligator's inevitable return. What was it Officer Wilde had said? Alligators are opportunistic lurkers. Dean climbed onto the paddle board, and headed toward Mrs. Triay's dock, using a two-by-four for an oar.

"Wait," Sabra called. "Something's come loose."

Stakes had fought free from the chicken wire. He wrestled them into place only to watch them slip away again. Water inched up the mangrove roots. Soon, it would be too deep to work. He tried another technique, pounding the stakes into the muddy river bottom with the two-by-four. But, by the time he secured one end of the barrier, the other side collapsed. Their masterpiece was sinking. A ribbon of daylight bloomed across the horizon. Water rushed through posts of a slat back chair. The tide had turned, dragging the ghost fence with it. Dean squinted toward the shadowy shore for Sabra. "Where are you?" he shouted.

A profound stillness answered. The sun breached Bird Island turning the sand a brilliant pink, and the oyster beds, a cobalt gray. The cuban tree frogs stopped barking. A solemn reverence to something or someone collapsed over the river, as if demanding Dean's silence. There, not ten feet away, the alligator's severe outline thorned the surface, steering past, breaking through the barrier with ease, settling beneath the safety of the mangroves.

Now, what? He couldn't tell Sabra he'd lost the fight. She'd be hysterical. But, there, from the darkness, came her voice, the gentler one. She didn't sound mad at all.

"Dean?"

"Sabra. Thank God," he said, relieved at the sound of her voice. He scanned the seawall. "Honey? Where are you?"

"Dean," she said. Her voice became a whisper, and then, a chorus of whispers. The sound of his name was like rain shelling tin. He followed the whispers into the cove. The dawning light made it difficult to focus. Everything was grainy. He should go back, take refuge at Mrs. Triay's dock. But, the whispers were insistent. They tugged like the somber cry that drew him here that night from his hammock. Maybe the whispering was part of the alligator's act. Dean paddled closer. Maybe all along the alligator had only wanted to help. The mangrove roots were fully underwater now. The whispers grew like pelting hail. The water glowed with the rising sun. The alligator stared with statue eyes, trying to tell him something. Dean eased off the board, and into the cool water.

The alligator struck quickly, an electric pain rising through Dean like lightning. He fought until he could no longer hear the whispers, until the water turned red and gold, until he had been swallowed whole.

When Dean could move again, his new body was an ancient costume of leathery bones. The wide tail propelled him forward like a rudder. The underwater landscape was gauzy through these strange eyes. A familiar roar, the one that brought him here that lonely night, rolled forth from his mouth. His body quivered against the dancing river. There was Sabra before him—her eyes fiery, her hair wild. The knuckles of her smooth, soft fingers that once traced the map lines of Moses Creek were now armored with horned scutes. Her clawed feet dug through the water. Dean followed, certain she knew the way.

How to Draw a Circle

MY SMALL HOUSE AT THE EDGE OF Clement Solano's bird aviary was backed by a creek I'd never seen. I tried once, but it was impossible to reach; there was no trail. I stopped at the black winter mud and fought woolly gnats that spun from the raveled cedar branches.

At the end of my first two months in the North Florida woods, I should have started to feel at home. I should have stopped looking at my feet for snakes as I walked. I fibbed when my mother called from Birmingham and asked, "Joy, how do you live alone in the middle of nowhere? You don't mind the animals? How do you stand the dark?"

I never told anyone, but I was petrified. That must be how I survived those first weeks without Marcus. It was fear that replaced wishing I'd never left; fear that replaced wishing I'd been able to put up with him having a wife. Wild cats called from the black woods at night and once there was a chicken snake, six feet long like a potato vine, wrapped around a low limb outside my window. There it was— oily skin all honey brown, dangling in the sun like an ornament or a hose. I planted zinnias in a rustic bed but was afraid to pick them when another chicken snake stretched through the chain link fence, an egg or a rat or a tomato swelling along its spine.

Tripp Roberts at the feed store sold me a sack of sulfur, powdery and white.

"They'll never pass it," he said, when I told him I needed something to keep the snakes from the hen house. I drizzled a ring around my house. If I was a priest or a shaman, I could have chanted and burned bundles of rosemary. But I was a sinner. The snakes would surely drip from the limbs and eat their way through my artillery.

By January, it was cold in the Florida woods, a damp cold, and I helped Clement warm the bird cages with plastic sheets we stapled to wire mesh. Those nights were the worst. There was no heat in my cabin so I wore gloves, two sweaters and a wool cap. And, there was scratching. Tiny prickling in the ceiling. Once, after rains pounded the tin roof for days, braking to a humid fog, and I thought the culprit was gone, the delicate slicing overhead continued. I followed its sound through the rooms and slapped the ceiling with a sandal.

Snakes hate sulfur, Tripp had said, but what about the rats I wanted to know. Do they hate? On those cold afternoons, they scampered up the leaning poles into the cages of Blue and Gold Macaws. They picked apart the pumpkin seeds from the bowls of orange slices and kiwi. The rats couldn't sleep underfoot of the birds. Soon, they retreated to my roof.

Every evening, the Maluccan Cockatoos and Lories and African Greys squawked at the approaching nightfall as if they meant to battle the setting sun. The sound was deafening. Four Greys could speak, and they mimicked Clement's cracker accent, "Where's Clement?" and "I love Barbara." And those who had no words screeched and screeched.

The peacocks, all twenty of them, honked their way single file into the fattest, tallest water oak, zigzagging across the limbs until finally they were in the highest place and darkness had fallen, leaving me to silence, to waiting. Only then could my cat and I pinpoint the scraping and whittling.

Maybe those were the worst hours. The waiting. Maybe those hours were worse than the cold hours because waiting reminded me of Marcus. Waiting for him to appear, waiting for him to acquire an open "window," as he'd called it—a moment of time when he could come to me unnoticed. But now waiting meant that I had time to consider what I had done. What I left was nothing that hadn't been left before. Everyone has left someone for someone else or a new place. This one was named Marcus and good, oh so good, and I missed him. If he hadn't been married, he'd have been even better.

Now waiting left me with the memories that had plunged their feet into my brain, decayed there like leaves. Rotten is not necessarily bad,

I told myself, as I discovered the biting sounds now came from the ceiling panel directly over my bed. You have to know when to leave it.

Solano Aviary was twenty miles from the nearest town and two miles off Don Manuel Road. There were no street lights. Sometimes, I would leave my car lights on for comfort, running out to turn them off after a half hour or so, hoping not to drain the battery. Out there, far from town, darkness was different. I couldn't grasp it like the tame, lonely darkness that looms in your own home. The kind that you recognize step after step and turn. This darkness was hollow. Before I left, I asked Marcus how long he thought it would take for things to blow over. Would his wife forget the things I told her? When could I come back to Birmingham? Darkness is a coward unable to answer.

The creek, Clement said, was called Moccasin Branch, not for the water moccasin or the cottonmouth, he assured, but for the shape the banks had formed over the years, a small, soft slipper of an Indian's shoe. In Alabama, water moccasins were known to chase you in the river and even along the bank. Once my mother went to the Winn Dixie for five pounds of Golden Russet potatoes, put the burlap in the sink, and the bag slithered across the drain.

Then, came the night when the scratching over my bed broke through to a hole the size of a pencil point. I knew it was only a matter of time, so I saluted the cat whose growls had grown deep and sinister. I went out into the dawn to the waking birds. The peacocks traveled down from their roost and one at a time straddled the hood of my Fiesta and pecked away at their blue and green images in the windshield. They had to see themselves Clement liked to say, or they would go mad. Upon my return, the rat lay on the end of my bed, a single puncture to its belly. I corked the ceiling hole with steel wool and masking tape.

After that night, I wrote Marcus. I gave him my phone number, my address. Joy Stokes, 2108 Solano Road, Elkton, Florida. I begged him to call.

Unable to speak, he sent letters. I kept them in a drawer till there were five, thick and bound with a rubber band. I imagined the scrubby blue print, the smears, the rhymes he'd make with my name.

My joy toy. Boy oh joy. Joyful noise. I loved the letters as they were. The magic would be gone when I opened them, I knew that, but I couldn't wait any longer. I sat facing the open fields at sunrise, spider webs dewy and sparkling in the light. I read them slowly.

"Please write more. I'll take anything. Even a letter bomb," he wrote, confessing that as he put pen to paper he was in an odd position. "Your favorite. Up against the hood of my truck."

But the truck wasn't parked in our secret spot at the end of Vulcan Road on the Alabama River in the dark. He wrote that he was in Mountain Brook posing for the Jefferson County Art League.

"I'm fully clothed, too. For a change," he said. "Levi's, a new yellow sweater. Canary yellow."

I WAS OFF ON MONDAYS AND SO WAS MY friend Cindy's boyfriend. Wayne drove out to my house with beer, some dope and a pipe he fashioned from a tool he stole at Ace Hardware where he worked in Gardening. He walked the perimeter of my rooms and said he'd like to go shoot pool, or maybe it would be best not to drive anywhere at all.

Wayne stared at stacks of papers on the kitchen table. "You write?"

"Poems," I said.

"About what?"

"Nothing."

There was no way to explain them. Marcus just knew. Marcus knew because they were him. Suddenly, the presence of the poems by the typewriter irritated me, like a stack of Florida Power and Light bills I would never be able to pay.

We took beers on a walk through the gardens. I pointed out the birds I knew, the ones Clement had taught me, and made up names for the rest. Customers milled around choosing their birds, trying to make them talk. Wayne and I sat in the barn and fed Susie, the pink Cockatoo, and she sang to us in her sweet baby voice. I liked to watch her claws move like fingers when I passed sunflower seeds to her. An old Playboy cover, the pale face of a green-eyed woman, looked up from the littered floor of Susie's cage.

At dusk, inside the house, Wayne played my guitar, but he only knew Buffet, and I didn't have the heart to tell him how much I hated the Keys and margaritas and that fantasy pirate life of a sailor shit. We drank all my beer and all his, and the light faded and with it came the flood of noise.

"I get the feeling something's about to happen here, what you think?" Wayne smiled. He'd put down the guitar.

I toyed with the rip in the knee of his jeans. Wayne was thin, about my height, and I thought I could probably wriggle into his Levi's. I could have never worn Marcus' jeans. He was built like a linebacker. Once, while I was still in Birmingham, and he had found a small window, I'd tried on his jeans and we'd laughed about how much joy could fit inside them. As he pulled his shirt overhead, I snatched his underwear from the pile on the floor and put them on. I was amazed at how good they felt. "These are now mine," I announced, modeling them for him. "You will not be getting them back."

He said he liked leaving them on me, and slipped the jeans over his bare skin.

Later, from a pay phone behind the liquor store near his house, he called and told my machine, "I can't believe you're out there in the wild wearing my BVD's."

The rooms in my Florida house grew dark. "Where's Clement? Where's Clement? I love Barbara," the African Greys called.

"Damn birds," Wayne said. He leaned to kiss me.

OUTSIDE, THE PINK WINTER LIGHT FADED over the macaw huts. The stubborn creatures fought on as if it were all a contest and the loudest might bring things to a halt and the day would miraculously stop there, just before its end, so we could all pause and rethink our plans, maybe ask for something more.

Spillway

TOLLY HAD BEEN WITH HER GRANDMOTHER, Lib, two months, and she had quit pestering for her mother's whereabouts. All she knew was the woman had found trouble again, this time a man ten years her junior. Before Tolly was grown and on her own, there would be more of her mother's men, long lists of them, but the one she'd discover that night would change her life forever. They were in Lib's tiny kitchen on Dubose Road, an assembly line of sterilized metal lids and wide-mouth Ball jars spread across the red Formica countertop, June Gold and Starlite peaches in bentwood bushel baskets on the floor. Lib was a telephone operator, had been for 35 years, and Tolly loved to quiz her on prefixes of towns across South Alabama. Lib bragged she never used the spiral-bound phone directories at work, and Tolly took full credit.

"Sehoy." Tolly said.

Lib clapped her hands. "245," she said. "Yes, indeedy. I'm on a winning streak."

For their game, Tolly had chosen Conecuh County just south of Mozelle, a land of orange mud and swift rivers. The Conecuh ridge where bootleggers hid, was known for illegal whiskey, a heavy port with an apple tang, fire-charred in oak barrels. This sloping forest is where Tolly suspected her mother, Janie, was wandering with a man she'd chosen over flesh and blood.

"Old Melton," Tolly said, thinking of the vine-swathed community at the base of a hill—a one-room schoolhouse, the gas station and country store run by a black man named Goliath. She imagined Janie sitting out back of a leaning clapboard house, a bonfire smoldering inside a rusty metal ring.

Sinking a June Gold the size of a grapefruit into boiling water, Lib didn't blink. "That's 377." She lifted the dripping fruit with tongs, carefully set it down on a dish towel. "Can't fool this old girl."

With sharp tweezers, Tolly slit a backbone along the scalded fruit, then skinned the peel, a steaming velveteen, all the while thinking of birthdays her mother missed, mainly the most recent, her fourteenth. When the telephone rang, Lib laughed at the timing of it; Tolly braced.

Lib nodded at the phone on the wall. "Mind getting that?"

With each use, the phone's spindly cord had knotted, entangling itself worse than the time before. Unraveling green kinks, Tolly said, "Hello?"

The husky alto asking for Elisabeth Gentry was from another world, bronze as scuppernongs. Tolly straightened her back. "Yes ma'am. She's right here."

Lib turned off the front eye of the stove; metal rings twirled across the Formica like toy tops. Whispering into the receiver, she headed into the hallway as far as the crimped cord would take her. The door closed.

From the front steps, Tolly squinted at the nosy headlights of a maroon Lincoln Continental. Lib leaned into the driver's side. Every October, when the concrete cooled, Lib repainted the carport floor a new shade; this year, dark Christmas holly. Tolly felt something with the toe of her Keds, and squatted to find a Matchbox car, a shiny gold Thunderbird. The car had belonged to Tolly's Uncle Sy; Lib kept them in a shoe box under the bed. In the dark, the women were arguing. Tolly couldn't make out the driver's face, but she would never forget the voice from the phone call.

"You can't bring the girl," the woman said.

"It's close to midnight. I won't leave her by herself."

Tolly tucked the Thunderbird into her shorts pocket. She still loved to roll the tiny cars. Lib went to the kitchen for her house keys, flipped on the porch light, and motioned for Tolly to follow. Tolly hesitated.

Lib pressed the small of her back. "It's okay. Get on in."

The woman Lib called Ramona held a sweating glass in her hand.

The amber liquid smelled oaky and sweet as banana pudding; the odor saturated the car. Neither of the women spoke as Ramona drove east, straight up the red-dirt road. They neared town, and there were street lights and orange clay splattering tires, skirting the underside of house trailers, staining bricks and clapboard cottages, white-columned antebellums; the clay did not discriminate. Tolly swore wherever she ended up as an adult, it would be where rivers did not taint soil. She yearned for white sneakers.

WHEN THEY ROUNDED THE MOZELLE town square, street lights illuminated Ramona's freshly dyed hair, perfect as a wig. She wore a tunic sparkling with glittering beads. Long sleeves in this weather? Tolly couldn't fathom it. The leather seat was sticky against her thighs.

"Where we going?" she asked.

Ramona lifted the glass to her lips and eyed Tolly from the rear-view mirror. Ice snapped against crystal. Tolly had heard the men in her family, before they all died or ran away, talk about how portions of moonshine from the ridge were set aside in oak barrels, a prized possession. The woman's eyes, hazel like Tolly's, glared as she took a calculated sip.

Lib turned to face Tolly. "Honey, we're looking for your mama."

They were driving away from Monroe County toward Wilcox County, weaving around deep ravines and gullies. She'd only been up to Camden, the county seat, once to see Lib's second cousin, Uncle Rouse. At times Tolly was eye to eye with the tree line and dramatic drop-offs. Her mother had run away off and on for years, but they'd never gone after her before.

"Why now? Has she sent word?"

"Yes," Lib said. "You could say that."

The familiar stillness between the two women, the stinging smell of bourbon, was suffocating. Tolly rolled down the window. She didn't like the idea of her mother unable to take care of herself. That meant she might come back, and Tolly had just begun to feel comfortable with the idea of staying at Lib's for good. On the other hand, she didn't want her mother gone forever.

"She's not dead, is she?"

Ramona gasped. Lib reached for Tolly's hand, and squeezed. "Honey, I don't know what we dealing with here. We just have word she might be needing us. That's all."

Tolly couldn't believe they were driving into the dense forests of Wilcox County when just an hour before they'd been laughing, and canning peaches. Lib promised weeks of peach pies, homemade peach ice cream, and rich preserves on their morning toast. Right before they started the prefix game, right before the phone call, Lib had wiped her palms on her apron, composed herself, scanned the countertop, and asked, "How we doing with our peach business?"

Lib referred to just about everything they were working on, and things that she might not be able to explain such as Tolly's mother's disappearances, failed love and lost dreams, family secrets that should be kept from others, as *business*. "How you coming along with that homework business?" Or, when Tolly was fibbing or holding back the truth: "You better stop all this funny business."

When Lib had begun to talk about the upcoming school year as that high school business, Tolly reminded her there were weeks ahead, far too many to think of ninth grade yet as a lingering *business*, though she had to admit when she did think of it like that, it was much more interesting than a bunch of kids learning Algebra 1 and Alabama history. For the rest of her life, Tolly would think this way, as if even monkey business, when handled correctly and carried out astutely, could indeed be a lucrative venture. She smiled to herself thinking of Lib, then remembered they were in a strange woman's car traipsing across Lower Alabama in the middle of the night. Why did her mother continue to disrupt her life even when she wasn't at home?

TOLLY DOZED, AND WOKE TO THE women bickering.

"All he said was he was going to the spillway," Ramona said. "He wanted to fix this once and for all."

Lib's arms were tightly folded across her chest. "If you'd got involved years ago, we wouldn't be here right now picking up the pieces."

Ramona finished off her drink, then set it between her legs. She looked straight ahead as she said, "Don't you tell me what I should have done."

"Ease up," Lib said. "There's the prison farm. Turn at that next road."

Hoops of razor wire lined the tall chain-link fences. Mercury lights flooded the grounds in sallow pink shadows.

Ramona slowed. "Good lord. They got all the lights blaring. How do those men sleep?"

"They're convicts. Nobody's thinking about their beauty rest."

Ramona turned down the long-neglected county road, tires gnawing shot gravel. The woods opened up to a broad clearing. Loblolly pines towered over concrete tables and barbecue grills.

Tolly sat up. The spillway. This was where the Alabama River had been dammed to create a shallow lake. Runoff stole over giant stone slabs, forming a wide slip-n-slide that had attracted children for years. "We use to have picnics here."

"Oh, honey. I thought you were asleep. That's right. The phone company's annual party was here for years."

"This is where Mama's at?"

"We're going to figure that out."

Ramona parked near the honor box. Its door dangled from a broken hinge. Tattered park admission envelopes littered the grass. Church's fried chicken buckets, Michelob and Schlitz bottles were strewn about. The spillway was on the other side of the levee, too dark to see. Tolly listened for water escaping.

Lib peered down at the lake. "They moved our cook-outs to Claiborne. For good reason." She gestured toward Ramona. "Flip on the headlights."

Yellow beams flashed the black water. A catfish surfaced, its whiskers piercing the surface. "I don't see anything or anybody. You drug us out here for nothing."

"Up yonder," Ramona said. "What's that?"

Tolly followed the women past a rotted out gazebo, a row of one-room cabins, the windows shattered.

Lib stopped. The headlights didn't reach that far, but the silhouette of an old model Dodge slumped at the bend.

"Stay here with Miss Owens. I'll be right back."

Tolly clung to Lib. She smelled of moth balls and Ivory soap. "I want to go back home."

"I won't be long. Now, you go on."

Lib jogged to the truck. The passenger side door groaned open. The dome light exposed the empty cab, beer bottles clanged to the ground.

"I remember coming here as a girl," Ramona said. "We used to slide down the spillway. You ever do that?"

Tolly felt for the toy car in her pocket. She didn't want to talk. Not now when her mother was lost, and the evening had been disrupted, but Ramona's voice was intoxicating.

"Yes ma'am. I did. The water's cooler than what's in the river dam."

"You know, the spillway's made of iron stone mined from this area. Great big slabs of it."

Tolly nodded. She thought of how the rocks were filmy and slick with river water. "There's a little island. You can walk across to the levee."

"I'd forgotten all about that. How about me and you come back here sometime? In the daylight, of course."

Tolly couldn't imagine doing such a thing, and was grateful when Lib reappeared before she could answer. Lib's long gray hair that had been tucked into a haphazard knot, was at her shoulders. She was out of breath.

"We got to call the sheriff."

"You know good and well we can't do that," Ramona said.

Lib handed Tolly a shoe. "Is this your mama's?"

It was a blue Keds, like her own. "I think so," Tolly said. "Where's the other?"

"I looked all over. Just found the one."

Lib held out a pair of scuffed men's loafers, dull brown. "What about these?"

Ramona clutched the shoes to her chest. "Oh, my God. They're Wendell's." She shouted out at the forest. "Wendell?" Her voice echoed. "Wendell! Where are you?"

"Who's Wendell?" Tolly asked.

Lib and Ramona locked eyes. Tolly held tight to her mother's shoe. The inside heel was damp and worn.

"Honey, you go on to the car," Lib said. "Wait for us there."

"But who is he?"

"Not now," Lib snapped.

Ramona stepped toward Tolly. "Let me explain"

"Don't you dare," Lib said.

Ramona's voice was calm and stern. "I have every right—"

"No, you don't. I am sick and tired of being told what to do."

"Elisabeth—"

"Calling me in the middle of the night? I've brought this little girl out here. I should be ashamed of myself."

Tolly walked away with the shoe. She imagined her mother hiking down gravel roads with one bare foot. Would she ever see her again? Up ahead she spied the water, the way the moon touched it now and then from behind a cloud. She reared her right arm back, and pitched the shoe as far as she could. The splash was loud and gratifying.

"Oh, no," Lib called. "Tolly?"

"She's okay. Let her go," Ramona said, and Tolly noticed something kind in her voice. It almost made her turn back. "Just let the girl be."

In the car, the smell of whiskey drenched the air. Lib had never spoken to Tolly so harshly. Tolly wished Ramona had never phoned them, that they'd never left their peaches. She climbed up into the front seat and opened the glove compartment. Behind the car manual, she found Ramona's registration, lifted it to the dome light. The address, 1439 Pecan Drive was in Mozelle, phone prefix 410. That was the tree-lined boulevard facing the county golf course. She thought of its white brick houses, glossy black shutters, and the broad covered porches tastefully decorated with sentinel urns of Boston ferns, wrought-iron café tables, varnished rocking chairs. Tolly put the registration back, stepped out into the damp night. The loblollies rose up in the distance, and she remembered discovering locust exoskeletons, abandoned and empty, clinging to their bark. By the water, the women's voices rose, and Tolly crept out of the car to listen.

"Do you swear to me that Janie did not call you?"

"Haven't heard from her in two months. Why would a mother lie about that? She missed that little girl's birthday."

"My other boys grew up good. They're all lawyers." Ramona went on about the one in Atlanta, the others in Birmingham, which one she'd need to call come daylight. "This one, Wendell. He's a real shame."

"They all wired different," Lib said. "That's all."

"He called me drunk and crying tonight. You understand what that's like?" Ramona said. "He told me he was going to see Janie. Said he was begging to see his baby daughter. He was crying. That boy a mine, crying."

The word daughter stung the air. Tolly bit her cheek, tasted blood.

"For years, I told you he could come and see her," Lib said. "For years. Anytime. And, you, too."

In the distance, water purred across the rocks. Tolly had asked who her father was, and every time her mother laughed, and from Lib she heard the same answer: "Family business." But hadn't she deserved to know? Tolly jumped from the shadows and raced toward the levee.

The spillway was not as smooth as she had remembered. Tolly took off her shoes and worked her way to the center, then sat down, stretching her legs on one of the slides that was filled with rushing water farther down. The stone scratched at her legs as she slipped her weight back and forth, gaining momentum, wondering where she'd end up when she let go. She couldn't recall where the slide ended, but it didn't matter. All she wanted was to be carried far away. Behind her, a match struck, and then her mother's voice. "Goddamn, girl, you trying to get yourself killed?"

"Mama?" she could barely make out her mother's figure from the shadows. She made her way back across at an awkward pace, maneuvering the sleek stone. "Are you okay? They're looking—"

"Shh," Janie said, and sat next to Tolly, who had pulled herself back up on the flat top of the spillway. "Last thing I need is those old ladies to come running."

Tolly attempted a hug, but Janie stretched her legs, revealing one bare foot. Janie saw her staring and wiggled her toes. "Where you think my shoe got off to?"

When Tolly didn't answer, she said, "So, you miss me?"

"Yes, ma'am." Tolly waited, but that was all.

Janie took a drag on her cigarette.

"Lib's worried."

"What else is new?" Janie grinned. "I've been watching y'all, waiting till those busybodies get done with their investigation. Then, I'm going to drive that truck out of the muck and meet up with Drake. He's the cutest thing. We got to get back to Cantonment before sunup."

"Cantonment?" That was the pulp mill town that smelled of rotten eggs, only twenty miles from the Gulf of Mexico. "You ever go to Pensacola?"

"About every other day."

At the thought of the squeaky sand and emerald water, broken sand dollars and butterfly shells, Tolly's heart fell. The last time she'd been there was third grade. And, to think, all this time she'd imagined her mother in Sehoy, drinking moonshine and driving reckless through oil country at night.

"Here's what we're going to do," Janie said. "You go on back to the car and keep this our little secret."

Tolly had never lied to Lib. "But, I can't."

Janie blew smoke toward Tolly, and then said slowly, "You will not ruin me."

Cicadas bleated from the pitch, and beyond that from the rutted road and the pink halo of the prison farm. Tolly didn't know how much longer she had before Lib found the two of them. "Is Wendell my father?"

Janie laughed. "You want to call him that."

"I been asking about my father. Why couldn't you tell me?"

For a moment the look on Janie's face said she might soften, but then she steeled again.

"Don't you go and cry on me. It wouldn't have done you a bit of good to know. And, it still won't."

Tolly wiped her face. "But where is Wendell now? We found a truck. Is he okay?"

"Oh, Jesus. That's Drake's truck. Wendell followed us. Drunk as hell, and Drake drove him back to town in his own truck, so he would't run off the damn road." The women's voices in the distance seemed panicked. Lib called for Tolly. "I went to see Wendell in Mozelle this afternoon is why he was drunk. I go ever once in a while to get a little money out of him, and he's always hoping for more."

"Child support?"

Janie grinned, reached for Tolly's hand, gave it a warm pat. "You always were a smart little thing."

The air grew damp. Tolly's wet clothes were heavy. She tied on her shoes, her feet dripping from the spillway.

Janie looked out toward the enormous loblollies. "When are those ladies going to give the hell up?"

"Mama?"

Janie turned to her, sighed. "What?"

Tolly took a deep breath. "You planning on coming back to town?"

Janie was close enough Tolly could see how her eye makeup was smeared. She seemed exhausted.

"I ran out on the rent," Janie said. "Maybe better to lay low a while."

Tolly nodded. The light had changed from deep black to gray. She couldn't hear the women, *her grandmothers*, anymore. she wondered what would happen if she went looking for Wendell on Pecan Avenue. She imagined the brick houses facing the golf course, with their automatic sprinklers and perfect turf grass. She imagined her mother, long ago, sneaking onto the hilly green with Wendell, barely out of range of the spigots. Or probably darting right through them. She looked up to see her mother studying her. Lib called out again, desperate.

"I got to go."

"Listen," Janie said. "Sometimes after work, Drake takes me over to the beach, and we swim and jump in the waves. Maybe one day I'll come get you. Would you like that?"

Tolly wondered if closing the distance between them was possible, if it was something she even wanted to do. "No, thank you," she said. "I don't think I would."

Janie shrugged, tamped out her cigarette. "Suit yourself."

"MY WORD," LIB SAID. "YOU'RE SOAKED to the bone."

"I went in the spillway."

"In this dark?"

Ramona brought a towel from the trunk. Tolly pulled it over her shoulders. It smelled of dog shampoo and flea powder. She looked out to the levee where her mother was hiding.

Lib opened the car door for her, kissed her head. "We couldn't find your mama. But, I'm sure she's just fine."

Tolly spread the towel on the seat. The backs of her legs stung with tiny abrasions. She dabbed the blood with the towel.

From the front seat Lib said, "You take a nap, and soon we'll be back to our peach business. We'll find everything just like we left it."

The June Golds and Starlites would surely be ruined by now. Lib's hand reached for Tolly, but she turned away and rolled down the window. In the pearly dawn, cicadas made their racket, and Tolly concentrated on the shadowy ditches and bramble ahead.

Visitation

FROM THE STAINED-GLASS WINDOW of Second Baptist Church in East Mozelle, Alabama, John the Baptist, bloody hair raging with serpents and fiery swords, glared down at Meredith Gentry with a wild look of disgust. Overcome with fear and nostalgia, Meredith looked away, and braced to greet her ex-boyfriend's family, or what was left of them. Tommy Billups's father overdosed on painkillers a few years back, and his mother hadn't made it a month past her cancer diagnosis. His parents never liked her. They blamed her for Tommy's carousing and overall bad luck. Meredith was relieved she wouldn't have to face them.

Hank, Tommy's younger brother, was first up. Meredith clasped his bear-paw hands. "Oh, honey," she said, careful not to let grudges of the past seep into her condolences. Hank seemed delighted to see her. The last time she saw him at his father's funeral, he'd given her the finger, and told her to go to hell. What a blow to discover your brother fallen out dead like that, she considered saying, but instead poised to offer a wise line about loss, she knew them well, such sweet proverbs and pithy poetics, but Hank was high as a kite, and mistook her for another woman.

"Alice," he said. "Sweet, beautiful Alice. Let me get a good look at you."

With nauseating effusiveness, he admired her from tidy ponytail to black blouse and pencil skirt. Meredith hugged on him to interrupt the awkwardness of the gawking.

"Good to see you, too, you poor, poor, fool," she said.

Eyes dilated, he smiled back.

"Idiot," she whispered, and moved on. She waited her turn at Julia, the eldest Billups sibling. Julia was worn and grayer since Meredith last saw her. She was speaking to an older, perfectly coifed, woman about how Tommy hadn't held a job in years. Meredith recognized the petite woman as Mrs. Haskew, her fourth-grade science teacher. She recalled the daily cloud journal she kept in her class, the glowing incubator of baby chicks, and the day Meredith announced to the class her dream of being a farmer, owning acres and acres of cotton and peas out on the Old Mexia Highway. Mrs. Haskew suggested she marry into a farming family, the likes of the Staceys or the Wiggins, or, him, they said, pointing to Tommy—son of a pecan farmer reclining in the back of the room working a spit ball against his cheek—and Meredith said, no, that's not what I mean. I want to *be* a farmer, and the whole class roared with laughter. Meredith turned so Mrs. Haskew wouldn't recognize her. She stared at the altar flowers, elegant sprays of white gerbera and red roses propped on easels. It was a miracle she'd even made it to the funeral.

She'd been running late, primarily because of the blinding rainstorm and traffic congestion on Interstate 10, but also because of the overwhelming dread that festered on the seven-hour drive to Alabama. It had her lingering at gas stations wondering what might happen if she turned around and went back to Gainesville. And, when she finally arrived in Mozelle, she'd driven through the old neighborhood for a good thirty minutes, allowing plenty of time for sour feelings to boil to the surface.

She'd almost missed the news of Tommy's death. A friend of a friend on Facebook, who like Meredith had long moved from Mozelle messaged her the obituary along with this note: "All I know is Hank's the one that found him." Meredith assumed a heart attack, as unhealthy diets and bad tickers were deeply seeded in the Billups family tree. But from the two women in line in front of her with their whispering and raised-eyebrow innuendos, she gleaned that Tommy fell from the deer stand at the family's hunting camp. He died alone, a silver-plated whiskey flask by his side. She stepped up to the pair discussing Tommy's demise, "You sure that's true?"

The red-haired one giggled. "Why wouldn't it be?"

"Jesus," Meredith whispered.

The women continued, heads together, voices quieter now; Meredith strained to hear. Hank didn't discover Tommy until two days after the fall, dried blood caked at his ears. Poor Hank, she thought. Poor, Tommy. Between the women's cavalier smiles and the image of dead Tommy, she felt sick to her stomach. She smoothed a loose hair, and fidgeted with the sleeves of her dress. The wait to speak with Julia was killing her. How long was this going to take? As per tradition in Wallace County, Alabama, this was the pre-service visitation, not to be confused with the viewing. That somber, and sometimes drunken event was at the funeral home the night before— Johnson's out on the bypass—where Tommy's body was displayed for family only, in one of the small velvety chapels. Meredith had moved from Wallace County ten years ago, so long ago she'd almost forgotten the rules. As she stood waiting her turn, she wondered what else she'd forgotten.

She did remember that deer stand. It was the very one Meredith had climbed out of on her first and only hunting trip with Tommy twenty years ago. The cautious doe crept to the salt spit, on high alert, scanning the meadow, and into the woods, checking right, then left, and right again, before bowing for the magnificent salt. Meredith watched Tommy grin, and raise his rifle. A sense of anger and wild injustice ran through her at the thought of what was about to happen. She grabbed Tommy's arm, shoving the gun away, and screamed. The deer leapt through sumac and smilax and bounded down a red-dirt road and out of sight. Tommy called Meredith a vegan bitch. Meredith wasn't a vegan back then, nor was she by any means a bitch, but twenty years later, she sure as hell was both now.

Of those ahead of her in the visitation line, she didn't recognize a one of them, except a man she recalled from the hardware store on the town square. He had a kind face, and a booming voice, and she wished she could recall his name. "Hi-dy," he said with a nod, before he embraced Julia. She was about to return the Hi-dy when Julia saw her, and stepped away from him, and said to Meredith, "Why are you here?"

"Oh, Julia. I'm so sorry to hear about Tommy."

"I bet you are."

Julia surely didn't say what Meredith thought she'd said. The chatter from the pews of mourners was getting to her. For the past few months her right ear rang when there was a lot of noise in a room. Her dive instructor explained the phenomenon was common for people who spent most of their days underwater. Meredith believed she didn't spend enough of it below the surface. She pressed her hand on her ear, as if that might stop the buzzing. For a crowd of mourners, they sure as hell were boisterous. "Pardon?"

"You heard me. Why *did* you bother coming here?"

Cold-hearted guilt was what hauled Meredith up at the crack of four a.m. to drive seven hours in the pouring rain. She thought if she came to her hometown, and paid respects, that the feelings that haunted her might go away, that there might be, as cliché as it sounded, some sort of closure. Obviously, she was wrong. "I came to say I'm sorry for your loss?"

"And, is it making you feel better?"

Meredith felt the sting all the way down to her proper black pumps. Julia's tirade had gotten the attention of a woman dabbing her eyes with a tissue. They'd gone to school with that woman. Shelby, Sheila, Sheryl? which was it? Julia was waiting.

"Not as good as I thought it would. That's for damn sure," she said. There was far too much gaiety in that church room full of mourners. She started down the steps to find a seat. It was a mistake to have come.

Julia grabbed her arm. "You're not leaving." She held her cellphone out, screen first, to Meredith. "Tommy and me were texting right before he died. You know what we were talking about?"

Meredith's right ear buzzed. She pressed on it, and squinted toward the cellphone.

"*You*," Julia said, putting the phone back in her pocket. "We were talking about you."

A crowd had formed around Meredith—Hank, Julia, Mrs. Haskew. The Billups were tall, pear-bodied people, and they loomed over her, their eyes widening. Petite Mrs. Haskew disappeared in their presence. And, where was that sweet man she saw? Hi-dy, she wanted to say. Hi-dy.

"You want to know what Tommy told me?"

The others glared, waiting. Meredith's mouth went dry. The room spun. There went her ear again. She felt woozy. To keep from fainting, she kept her focus on the powder blue carpet, and the matching velveteen cushions that lined the mahogany pews she'd sat in since she was a child. There'd been few renovations over the years. But the baptismal, a square pool above the choir loft, was now barricaded with high glass walls. There was a hint of chlorine in the air. She remembered climbing those steps as a young girl, peering down into the cool water wearing a white robe, ready to drown her sins. At the time, she hadn't accumulated enough to rinse away. If there had only been insurance on what was to come.

"You want to know what he told me, don't you?" Julia said.

Julia's piercing eyes said she had the upper hand. The truth tended to boost one's confidence. Meredith stepped back slowly. No, she didn't want to know, nor did she want to see those text messages, but she couldn't make her mouth work. The pianist began the opening bars of, "*What have I to dread, what have I to fear/Leaning on the everlasting arms?*"

To Meredith's amazement, she began to hum along as if she had that worn Baptist hymnal in her hands. The song was a comfort, and it gave her strength, and for a moment reminded her of who she truly was—not the callous woman Julia had implied—but when she looked out at the crowd for affirmation, at the people she had known since she was born, they were strangers. As the pianist played on, the crowd ceased its chatter, acknowledging it was time to get down to the business of honoring the dead. Julia removed the phone from her pocket and held it out to Meredith until the pastor stepped up on the stage, and led the family down to the front-row pew.

MEREDITH SCANNED THE CROWDED PEWS. The sun disappeared behind the clouds, darkening the stained glass. She couldn't imagine sitting through the service. Avoiding the now sultry eyes of John the Baptist, she walked down the aisle, and kept going. If she remembered correctly, there was a door in the corner that led into a coat room, and then a narrow flight of dark stairs into a basement, unheard of in this floodplain. Taking chances in the name of the Lord, she remembered her mama saying, as she leaned back in a deck chair in their back yard, knocking cigarette ashes off into her brother's baby pool, freckling the plastic boats and ducks before the toy fire brigade took over. The last flood Meredith remembered in Wallace County was when she was eleven or twelve. Sunday school chairs floated upstairs into the sanctuary, and an older man was whisked away atop a jon boat. For long as she could remember grainy, orange watermarks lined the walls like the crayon height measurements on the kitchen door frame of their old house on Loblolly Lane. Meredith tried the door; it was locked.

She remembered another door that led down further into a strange array of classrooms with Dutch doors. It smelled of graham crackers and grape juice. She passed a line of rain coats on hooks, and as soon as she saw a package of Pall Mall Lights poking out of a pocket, she couldn't turn away. Upstairs, the hymn was in its final, dramatic bars. She reached into the pocket, shook out three cigarettes, and then a fourth for good measure. She dug deeper into the pocket, and found a green Bic lighter. Satisfied, she flung open the door, and stepped outside, a carpet of damp pine straw underfoot.

The giant pine trees were soaked to the bone, the bark so black that the green against it was a brilliant technicolor. She squinted and found her sunglasses. The odor was part balsam, part nostalgia. Meredith inhaled. It took her back to the morning she'd alerted the deer of Tommy's gun. She'd wandered off into the woods alone wearing an orange cap and jacket. She knew Tommy would be angry, so she'd give him time to calm down. She located the brook Tommy had taken her to before hunting season when it was safe to follow its meandering curves, but now in November in the Alabama woods, *she* felt hunted. Meredith made sure to whistle, and do jumping jacks and make un-deerlike noises all the while. It was terrifying, and just about every man in Mozelle was in the woods that weekend. She'd intended to cool off, splash about in the little creek, and then hike back up and apologize to Tommy. They would then, more than likely, get on with their lives, marry, have children, and learn to put up with this one cultural difference that they had, but by the time she had walked out of those woods, and back into the clearing, facing the salt spit, it was to tell Tommy she didn't want to ever see him again.

Now, standing beneath the pine trees on the church grounds, she felt a sudden chill up her spine, but she wasn't in the dark woods on hunting land. She was safe.

"Well, looky here," said a voice from behind. "If it ain't—"

Meredith jumped, suppressed a scream, and turned to see her old friend, Gayle.

"Damnit," she said, throwing her arms around her. "You liked to scared me to death."

Gayle stepped back, and looked Meredith over. "Looking fine, girl." She hugged her again. "Now, give me one of them cigarettes."

Meredith handed her one; Gayle motioned she light it.

"Sure is good to see you," Meredith said again. Those hymns inside the church, with their clanky chords and pleading stanzas, gave her breath, but this voice of Gayle's, coy and silly, and full of secrets, gave her life.

"You came all this way, but didn't listen to the service?"

Meredith laughed. "Miss high and mighty. I don't see you in there, either."

"Oh, honey, we all know it's the graveside that gets you the points."

"Points?"

"Brownie points. I've racked them up over the years. Then, if I need anything? I pull my points. So graveside, most folks leave, go on home. They think they've done their duty after the church service. But not Anna Gayle Steele. I'm somebody you can count on." She winked. "Plus, *that*?" she turned all the way around to face the church. "They've probably got the slide show going about right now. Newborn Tommy, Toddler Tommy. Emotional tenderizer. That's the last thing I need right now." She grinned, and slowly turned back to Meredith.

"Well, it's good to see you," Meredith said. "Now, I'm glad I came." She thought of Hank, Julia, the cellphone, and cringed. "If I only had a stiff drink."

"*If?* Who do you think you're talking to?"

Gayle walked off across the dirt lot to her Chevy Cavalier. It was an old model but in good shape. Blue, her big brother, was certainly still in the auto business from the way that thing was buffed, and shined, the prettiest pearl matte blue she'd ever seen.

Meredith laughed as Gayle strode back with a flask in a leather cover, with two silver shot glasses. She unscrewed the top, filled both to the rim. "Oh, Gayle, I was joking. I can't. I've got to drive to Tallahassee this afternoon."

The confident veneer of Gayle's expression broke, and there was a flash of something deeply lost and sad in her eyes, but she recovered and smiled, and handed Meredith a glass. "Oh, don't be such a baby."

Meredith wanted to explain how she's planned an evening with old college friends, how she looked forward to talking about their common work on the invasion of algae and non-native species in North Florida freshwater springs. But she knew Gayle, and it would all sound pompous to her. This was the effect Gayle and half of Mozelle, for that matter, always had on her, that her own opinions and dreams and fears didn't matter, and then there was that strange encounter with Julia, and the overall feeling of what she had escaped, and what Gayle hadn't, that did it. She reached back, and downed the shot. It was bourbon. Hot, invigorating, and stunning on the down take. "Damn." She looked up, suddenly remembering she'd not asked Gayle how she was doing at all. "I was sorry to hear about your mother."

Gayle shrugged. "Thanks," she said. She dropped her cigarette, and turned the ball of her foot on it. "I had to go back home to live with Daddy. You know, after Ben—"

Meredith nodded. "I heard. I'm so sorry."

"Well, after he ran off with the lovely Mrs. Watson—" Gayle's voice drifted; she eyed the flask. It was the kind all Wallace County High seniors were given at graduation—stainless steel, six ounces, monogrammed. Meredith wondered where hers was—in an unpacked box, no doubt. "I just couldn't stand being in that house by myself. So, I sold it. And, you know what? I'm going on a cruise to the Bahamas this summer."

"Good for you." They clinked empty glasses. "You do know they deserve each other."

Gayle leaned against a pickup truck. She sighed. "Least I got my boys."

"I'd love to see pictures."

She reached into her purse. "They're doing real good. Despite their father being a you-know-what. Ray's in middle school. JB's doing little league. Freshman, high school. God help me."

The younger boy had Gayle's grin, his wide green eyes. "Damn, he looks just like you. They're both so handsome." She meant it. They were adorable.

Gayle beamed. "Thank you."

"Living with Daddy's not too bad," she volunteered. "He keeps to himself. Mostly glued to that damn TV. He can't remember his own name, though. I hate to imagine what comes next." She laughed, started to elaborate, but the front door to the church had flung open, along with a sudden burst of piano chords with such finality to them that it took Meredith's breath away. The service was over. And, as her grandmother would say, they'd sung Tommy on to "meet his eternal reward."

"Well, shit," Gayle said, gathering her things. "Short and sweet. Come on. Ride with me." They got in the Chevy, and Gayle reached back into the glove compartment for the flask. "One for the road." She offered another round.

Meredith considered saying no to a second, but then she thought of the Starbucks in Crestview at the interstate. She'd stop for a double espresso on the way out of town, and sober up. She did have to face Tommy's family again at the graveside. Maybe this shot would even out her emotions. "Cheers," she said.

THEY WAITED IN THE CAR UNTIL the others began to snake their way in a long procession of vehicles toward the cemetery down by the river, and then Gayle waited until the highway patrolman motioned her into the line.

"Tell me," Gayle said. "Why didn't you suffer, I mean," she laughed at her own joke, "sit through the service?"

Meredith looked out the window. How could she explain it? "I don't know."

"You drove all this way to steal a few cigarettes?"

Said like that, it did sound ridiculous. It was a long damn drive for nothing. She wondered now if she was making too much of a deal about what Julia said. "The weirdest thing happened back in the visitation line."

"Lay it on me, girlfriend."

All along the red-dirt road, the ditches were flooded, and through the pine trees, the muddy river was frothy and orange. It must have been raining hard for days. She could feel Gayle's eyes on her, waiting for an answer. Julia's announcement hit at something she'd tried to avoid all these years. She didn't know how to even begin to explain it. "Oh, never mind. It was nothing."

"You say so," Gayle said. They parked on the side of the road, and walked along the gravel paths, higher ground between the headstones, to dodge swaths of slick red mud. "Why they built a cemetery here, I'll never know."

Up ahead, the pastor was already reading a selection of verses. Meredith stopped in her tracks at the scene. The family sat in folding chairs covered with black velveteen. There were huge wreaths of white roses and gladioli, and an enormous spray at the casket of red and white chrysanthemums over a herringbone ribbon. Her eyes welled. Tommy was a Roll Tide fan through and through. She straightened, and told herself it was the bourbon talking.

"Come on," Gayle said, tugging on her arm. "We'll miss it."

The rain had turned the red clay to a slick paste. Gayle's three-inch heels sunk so deep into the mess, she looked like she was wearing flats. "Shit," she said, a little too loud. From the graveside, heads turned. She whispered, "I look like a whore in a graveyard."

Meredith put her fingers to her lips. "Hush," she said, but her foot slipped, and Gayle grabbed her forearm. "Jesus, you're going to take us both down." The way they were leaning against each other reminded Meredith of the time they went ice skating in the Montgomery mall. They'd spent more time on the ice than not. Gayle's grip tightened. Meredith whispered. "We should have gone that way," she said, pointing to another path leading to the tent and Tommy's casket. With that, Meredith felt her left leg slip. She recovered, but the weight on her arm from Gayle's tugging caused her to lose her balance. Just as she stepped forward, her foot skidded across the slick mud, and she fell, bringing Gayle with her. They screamed. The crowd beneath the tent turned to see them. Someone yelled, "Quiet." The preacher went back to his solemn recitations.

Meredith carefully maneuvered to a kneeling position to assess the damage. People in the back of the tent turned around.

"I'm going to have to throw these shoes away," she said.

"My dress," Gayle said, looking at her frayed, muddy hem, and broke into laughter.

An awkward pause followed by a reverent round of amens, and then, probably earlier than planned to drown out the laughter, the pastor began the opening bars of "Amazing Grace."

"Let's go say hi to Hank," Gayle said. "I feel bad as shit for him."

"No thanks. I'd rather not."

"Party pooper." She fished the keys from her purse, and tossed them to Meredith. Behind them, a voice boomed. It was Julia.

"You two always were nothing but trouble," she said.

Gayle, not even bothering to turn around to confirm that it was Julia, winked at Meredith. "Hey, speak for yourself," she said as she brushed dried mud off her sleeve.

"I was not finished talking to you," Julia said pointing at Meredith.

Meredith clung to the car keys. "I need to get out of here."

Hank wore the herringbone casket sash draped over his shoulder like a beauty queen. "Hey," Hank said, suddenly sobered, and pointing at Meredith. "She's not Alice."

Gayle whispered. "Who the hell is Alice?"

Hank yelled, nearly hysterical. "She told me she was Alice."

Gayle tugged Meredith's arm, and they made their way across the mud. Julia caught up with them. "Trying to pull one over on us, huh?"

"I'm Meredith Gentry for God's sake. Who else would I be?"

Gayle whispered. "There's no reasoning with that shit. Let's go."

Julia hollered. "Trying to trick my baby brother. You know he's not well."

With that, Hank's shoulders heaved, and Julia led him toward a path of graves. He knelt over and wretched.

"I'm not done with you," Julia called across the cemetery. "I'm not. I'm not done."

MEREDITH AND GAYLE WRAPPED THEIR filthy shoes in plastic Winn Dixie bags. Barefoot, Gayle started the car. She warmed her palms over the heat vents. "Well, some things never change. Julia's still a bitch. And, that poor Hank—"

Meredith shuddered. "What's wrong with him? He always had been a little off."

Gayle tapped her temple, and reached for the glove box. "Four-wheeler. Knocked some more of those screws loose. He's doped up most of the time." She held out the flask and shot glasses.

The mud and Julia's cross words had irritated Meredith, but this news about Hank on top of the irreverence that Gayle had shown at the graveside fiasco infuriated her. She waved the drink away. "My God, Gayle. No."

Gayle slammed the glove box. "You know what? I always wished you would loosen up a bit."

There was silence in the car. This time they didn't have to wait their turn. The others had lingered to pay respects. Meredith felt defeated. She'd come all this way and had not even begun to redeem herself. And, she'd made Gayle mad. Meredith glanced at her watch. She'd been in Mozelle all of three hours. What a disaster. And, she couldn't deny the fear that was building. She felt helpless.

"Gayle?"

Gayle looked at her, curious, as if she remembered that desperate tone. When they were twelve, Gayle talked her into shoplifting green apple Now & Later candy from the Red and White Grocers. Officer Dailey had separated them—Gayle in the front of the patrol car, Meredith in the back—the glass divider between them. Meredith had never been in trouble. She remembered the cigarette smell engrained in the vinyl seats. Head in her hands, she'd closed her eyes. All she could see was prison time. It was Gayle who explained it was a rouse. "Act sorry," she'd said through the speaker vent. "And then they'll let us go."

They were both in the front seat now, that glass divider replaced by a more complex, invisible one.

"What?" Gayle said. "Spit it out. What's going on?"

Meredith looked out the window. There was something about the sentinel pines and red dirt that always got to her, made her feel at home. "What happens if you're the last person someone speaks to right before they die?"

With the same authority she'd delivered from the front seat of the patrol car years ago, Gayle said, "It means they're trying to bring you with them."

Meredith gasped. "That's creepy, Gayle."

"Well, you *asked.*"

They were both quiet as Gayle drove into the parking lot. Now, more than ever all Meredith wanted was a strong cup of coffee and to get the hell out of Mozelle. It would be so good to get to Tallahassee and see her friends, but on second thought, she might drive straight home to Gainesville. Gayle's words had chilled her.

Gayle turned into the church parking lot, and they lumbered across the dirt lot. Gayle chuckled. "Well, my friend, you're not going anywhere anytime soon."

Assuming she meant the afterlife, and that no one was yanking her out of this world just yet, Meredith felt incredible relief. "Thank God for that."

"No," Gayle said. She had stopped the car, and was waving out in front of her. "I really mean it. You are not going *anywhere.*"

Before them was Meredith's almost unrecognizable Honda CRV. A six-foot limb from the pine tree overhead had fallen and gutted a hole in the windshield. Glass diamonds cascaded over the car.

GAYLE'S BROTHER, BLUE, ARRIVED in his tow truck a half hour later. He was still handsome, and wore his hair in a long ponytail, though he was now soft around the edges. Meredith noticed the shiny wedding band. Gayle had mentioned he divorced again, and remarried quickly. Meredith asked how long the repair would take.

"Soon as I get the parts. My guy's coming from Pensacola tomorrow. He'll bring it on the truck."

Meredith did the math. Pensacola was an hour and forty-five minutes away, depending on traffic. Oh, God, she'd be here another day, at the very least. "I can't possibly stay in Mozelle one more minute."

Gayle was on the phone with one of her boys, but said, "Well, excuse me."

She and Blue exchanged a look.

"I'll do what I can," Blue said. "As fast as I can."

GUILTY FOR HER REACTION TO BLUE'S OFFER, and for the fact that despite her rudeness, Gayle offered to put her up for the night, Meredith volunteered to buy dinner. She asked Gayle to stop at the Piggly Wiggly on the way to the house. Inside the store, she picked up a rotisserie chicken, mashed potatoes from the deli, a bagged salad, and a half-gallon of sweet tea. She'd do her best to salvage the night. It would be like two old friends catching up.

Gayle braked at a stop sign on Golf Drive. She nodded east. "Want to go by your old house?"

That morning, Meredith had driven down the street, pausing at the deep gully at the end of the road, and the still-empty lot of shoulder-high golden rod next door. "The house is for sale again. I went by earlier."

"Anywhere else you want to go? Memory Lane?"

Thinking about Tommy, and summer afternoons, all those times with him before things went bad, she said, "You know, I *would* like to drive by the lake."

The man-made Mozelle Lake was dug in the late 1950s, and until ten years ago, had served as the town's swimming hole. It sat at the base of a hillside of enormous azalea bushes, camellias, dogwoods, and pine trees, and as Gayle slowed at the far end of it where the road gave view to the hill, Meredith wished it was spring already. In April, the park would be a sea of pink and white and fuschia blossoms. Now, it sat dormant and expectant, quietly on the verge of change. As a teenager, this had been her hangout. Now, the surface was covered with duckweed and blue-green algae. As Gayle told a story, something about a new pool being built on the other side of town, Meredith scanned the shore, recalling floating on a flimsy, yellow raft. She'd offered Tommy her hand, and he'd scrambled atop the raft next to her. They'd floated far from the shore, a golden cascade of light embracing them.

"MY BOYS ARE AT BEN'S THIS WEEKEND," Gayle said, apologetic. "It'll just be me, you and Pop."

Gayle had been eager to show off the updates she'd made to the house—fresh paint and new tile to replace shag carpet. Pine flooring, along with the sunny south-facing windows gave the kitchen a festive look. She'd kept the faded Formica countertops with gold flecks. "They remind me of Mom," Gayle said, and shrugged, embarrassed of a show of sentimentality.

They ate dinner, and finished off the ice tea. They lingered at the table a while, laughing, telling stories. Finally, they gathered the dishes. Gayle washed, and Meredith dried plates and set them in the cabinet. She remembered where everything went, as if she'd never left. Mr. Steele came in and out of the room. Each time, Gayle reintroduced them. Meredith felt relaxed, at home. Why had she been so reluctant to stay the night, she thought?

As Mr. Steele headed to the living room again, Gayle said, "I've been thinking." She looked suddenly tired, dark circles shadowed her eyes. The tone in her voice had shifted. Meredith braced.

"When we left the cemetery?" Gayle continued. "You asked about talking to someone right before they died? What was that really all about?"

Meredith busied herself with the dishes, moving mugs around in the cabinet. "Nothing. I said it was nothing."

Gayle had grown impatient, her voice was strained. "You talked to Tommy, didn't you? That day. Before he fell out of the tree stand."

Meredith, feigning interest in the organization of coffee cups, said, "We did. We talked."

"About what?"

Meredith closed the cabinet door, and poured a glass of water. "Why do you care?"

"He loved you. You know that. And, he wanted you back here."

"And, if he'd had had his way?" Meredith said, thinking back to the deer stand years ago, "I would have been pregnant and married at seventeen."

"Like me?"

Meredith stared into her water glass. She kept sticking her foot in her mouth. "I'm going to bed," she said, though she didn't move.

"You know what?" Gayle said. "You did fine. Just because Mozelle and everybody in it tried to," she said, making quotation marks with her finger, "keep you from your dreams." Gayle slammed the refrigerator door, and marched from the room.

Meredith collapsed at the kitchen table, staring into the Formica, running her fingers over the gold flecks. She looked up to see Mr. Steele.

"Who are *you*?" he asked.

"To tell you the truth, I don't really know."

Satisfied with that, Mr. Steele nodded, and then poured himself a glass of orange juice. He thoughtfully drank it as he studied her, and walked off down the hall.

MEREDITH HAD BEEN ASSIGNED THE guest room off the kitchen, Gayle's childhood room, and it had not undergone renovations. There was the same pink shag carpet, the same dark wood paneling. Meredith looked under the bed, delighted to find the same box of Legos they played with as kids. She sifted through the plastic pieces, remembering hours constructing rigid rectangular houses and windowless towers. In bed, it seemed she had just drifted off when the sound of the pocket door rolling open woke her. Gayle had mentioned Mr. Steele sometimes roamed the house at night. "Mr. Steele? That you?" she said.

There was no answer, but a shadow blocked the doorway. She switched on the bedside lamp, and there, Tommy stood. Grinning, he closed the door behind him.

"My God," she said, snatching her cell phone from the bedside table. Who should she call? The police?

"Shh," he whispered. "Put that phone down. I don't want everybody in Mozelle getting all worked up."

He sat down on the end-of-the-bed bench, facing her. His grin was reassuring. Meredith relaxed. In a strange way, she'd missed him—the way he talked, the way he turned his head. It reminded her of the good times. She reached out to touch him; he eased back a little. "Is it really you?"

"Sure. I mean I'm dead and all, but it's me." His laugh was deep and infectious, unleashed from somewhere far, far away.

"Tommy, what're you doing here?"

He gave that familiar shrug, and a wide grin. His dimples appeared. "I'm supposed to show you something." He reached into his pocket, and held out a cellphone. It was Julia's, the neon green casing glowing in the dark. She remembered it from the funeral. "Come here," he said, motioning. "Closer."

Meredith crawled up to the end of the bed, covers falling to the side. Tommy hit the light button on the phone, and held it to her face. The letters were glittery and blinking but it was no doubt what they said: YOU'RE NEXT.

She jumped back. His face turned to a scowl. His arms were claws, and he growled, and roared, and Meredith scrambled into the headboard. A scream lodged in her throat, and there she was sitting up in bed, the covers neatly across her legs. The bench was in its place. It was 6 a.m. Tommy was gone. From the kitchen came the aroma of coffee, and the gurgling growls of the percolator.

MEREDITH DRESSED QUICKLY, WASHED HER face with cold water, and stared at herself in the mirror. She was alive. Wasn't she? She pinched herself until she thought she might bleed. That was a dream. Tommy was dead. *You're next.*

In the kitchen, she prepared to reintroduce herself to Mr. Steele, but he looked straight through her. "Good morning, Mr. Steele. It's Meredith. Remember me?"

He poured coffee into a red mug, and looked out the window, sipping it.

"Mr. Steele?"

Meredith pinched her arm. Tommy's face, clear as day, came to her from the night before. It was just a dream. Wasn't it?

She needed something stronger than coffee. It was too early for Gayle's flask. When Mr. Steele was done with the cream and sugar, she took her turn. She always drank her coffee black, but suddenly wanted heaps of sugar. She picked up the *Mozelle Journal* and thumbed through it. As if she weren't even there, Mr. Steele grabbed the sports section from her hands, and wandered out the back door, leaving the kitchen door wide open. Cold air seeped in. Meredith got up and closed it behind him, her hands still shaking. Outside, Mr. Steele had settled into a wrought iron settee like it was a summer day. Did *"YOU'RE NEXT"* mean she'd be hit by a log truck soon as she drove onto the interstate, fall to the ground from a heart attack, or that she'd be plucked off the earth and vanish?

Meredith located the obituaries. There it was, "Thomas Wayne Billups." He was dead all right. Then, she gingerly traced her finger down the page, hesitating as she came to the G's, but there was no Meredith Gentry. She laughed at herself to keep from crying, and went to the funny paper. Cartoons, that's what she needed. She had another cup of coffee, and at 7 a.m., rummaged through her purse for Blue's business card, and phoned the garage. Blue wasn't there yet, the woman who answered told her, but she'd have him call her—what was this about?

"My car, a Honda CRV. The windshield's broken. Blue brought it in yesterday—"

"We don't have any cars here. It's just me," and she laughed. "And the garage cat. Diesel."

"But, Blue said his guy was coming from Pensacola. The parts will be on the truck—"

"No car. No truck. Just the cat."

"I was there. We brought it in—"

"No car. No truck. Just—"

Meredith hung up on her. She went to the room to gather her things, and checked herself in the mirror. Her hair looked atrocious, but it was her. Tommy's scent was in the air. Musky and tobacco like. My God, she had to get out of this house, and out of this town. She'd find a hotel. Was the Mozelle Inn out on the bypass still open? Down the hall, a door opened and closed. Water whooshed through the old pipes. Gayle came whistling into the kitchen. Meredith held out her arms. She turned a circle. "Can you see me?"

"Bigger than life. As always. Even *without* my contacts." After rifling through a cabinet, she chose an orange and blue Auburn mug. *War Eagle*, it said. Meredith was surprised as she watched Gayle make her coffee. No milk, no cream. Black.

Gayle sensing something, turned to her. "What's wrong with you *now*?"

"I called the garage about my car. It's not there. It's gone."

Gayle laughed. "You think somebody stole it?" She explained

that Blue towed it across town to his buddy's garage in East Mozelle. He's got the parts. "I was going to come tell you, but it was late when he called, and you'd been such a bitch. I didn't want to interrupt your beauty sleep. Believe me, they want to get you out of here soon as they can."

Meredith "Oh God. Thank God."

Gayle looked out the kitchen window, her eye on Mr. Steele. "I'm still pissed at you."

Meredith spooned more sugar into her coffee, and nodded. "I know."

"You look like shit," Gayle said. "What's wrong?"

Meredith sipped her sweet coffee. It was the best thing she'd ever had. Why had she avoided sugar all these years? "I had a rough night."

They sat at the table a while without speaking. Avoiding Gayle's eyes, Meredith said. "Tommy came to see me last night."

"What'd he want?" Gayle's matter-of-fact tone was reassuring, but the look on her face was devilish. She winked.

"He said: 'You're next.' "

Gayle didn't miss a beat. She smacked the table with her palm. "Well, then," she said. "Better get your shit together."

GAYLE DROVE MEREDITH TO THE GARAGE in East Mozelle. Meredith went inside to pay the bill, and when she returned, Gayle was at the car admiring the new glass.

"You think it's a good idea to go see Julia? After what happened yesterday?"

"Like you said. I got to get my shit together."

"Been a long time since someone took Anna Gayle Steel's advice." She laughed, but there was the sadness in her voice again. "Wish you could have met my boys."

"I do, too. Next time?"

"Girl, you're not coming back here."

She spoke like it was a declaration, a fact. Meredith tried to shrug it off. "How about ya'll come to Florida sometime? We'll take the kids to the beach."

Gayle shifted on her feet, and leaned against the car door. "Sounds like a plan," but the hype was gone from her voice. She may as well have been discussing mopping the kitchen floor. She mustered a smile, and ran her hand over the new windshield. "Now, you'll be able to see better."

The words hung in the air, and finally Meredith hugged her. She waved from the car, and tapped the horn—beep, beep, beep. In the rear-view mirror, Meredith watched Gayle's face, strong and wise, fade away.

INSTEAD OF HEADING TO BREWTON, AND then on to Crestview to take the interstate east, Meredith went back through Mozelle, toward Mexia, or Mexie, as is was known to its few residents. She drove through the four-way-stop, passed the skeleton of an old general store swallowed by kudzu, and slowed to find the BILLUPS PECANS sign. The black-top road quickly turned to red-dirt, and she drove deeper into the heart of Wallace County, where there was nothing more than pine forests crowding in all around, and Gayle's voice as loud as if she were in the car. "Get your shit together."

The road to the farm was flanked with kudzu-laden gullies. The desperate vines scrambled their way from these pits as if they were running from fire. Some choked telephone poles and inched to the road. Meredith let the windows down. Her knuckles reddened, and her nose ran, but the air was clean, and pure. Funny, she thought, but she *could* see a little better. The sky was clearer, cloudless, in fact. Finally, the clay and the vines gave way to wide fields of pecan trees, and clawing bare limbs. The modest brick house sat just off the road between the trees. An array of four-wheelers and boat trailers littered the yard. She parked out by the mailbox, as far as she could get from a tree. There was the old porch swing, flung on its side, and mountains of gathering baskets. The whole yard smacked with memories, all those days she'd sat for hours with Tommy, dreaming of what could have been. She thought of that last phone call. She had been so awful, so unkind.

AT THE FRONT DOOR, JULIA GREETED HER with a scowl, but the bravado from yesterday was gone. "What do you want?"

"Can we talk? Meredith said. "Before I go back to Florida?"

A cold wind blew Julia's skirt. Meredith shivered in her wimpy coat. Julia didn't budge.

"I shouldn't have left so soon yesterday. At the cemetery. But then Hank got sick, and Gayle—"

Julia sighed. "Hank's sleeping. We'll go out back," she motioned Meredith to follow her through the house.

The cramped front room was warm as a greenhouse; immediately Meredith's skin pricked with perspiration. Hank was asleep on the sofa, his mouth open. She wanted to wake him, trick him about this so-called Alice woman, but he winced in his sleep as if fighting off a bad dream. He looked weak despite his girth. Ashamed of herself, she followed Julia outside into the cold.

Outside, on a newly constructed deck, Julia sat on a lawn chair. She pulled her coat around her. The deck smelled of fresh pine and had built-in seating, and wide steps leading down to the pecan orchard. In straight rows, hundreds of pecan trees stood on guard.

"This is new," Meredith said, running her hand across the smooth railing. "It's nice."

Julia admired it, nodding. "Tommy built it."

Meredith hadn't known Tommy to ever build a thing. She gave a half-laugh, those very words in her mouth, as she glanced up at Julia. The woman's cross expression was a warning. As if she had never planned to say a thing, Meredith turned toward the acres and acres of pecan trees, line by line of them as far as she could see. She took a deep breath, and then stopped. God, after all this, she couldn't formulate what she had come here to say.

Julia crossed her legs, and made a ticking sound with her nails on the railing. "You come all the way up here to admire my trees?"

Meredith looked down at her hands. "So, Tommy had asked me to marry him."

"I know that. He forwarded me your text messages. Said you turned him down."

"But I hadn't seen him in years! We were not in love."

"It broke his heart all the same."

Meredith shook her head, exasperated. It was hard to believe he still loved her, after all that time. "So, he sent the message when he was up on the tree stand?"

Julia took her phone from her pocket. The gesture reminded her of what Tommy had done the night before, and it made Meredith's hands go cold. Julia scrolled through the messages. "Two or three in the afternoon is when he sent them to me. Right before he died. The coroner's guess."

Meredith cringed at the word coroner.

Julia returned the phone to her pocket. "You didn't love him. You said you didn't. Right there in the message. Just like that, you said, 'I don't love you.' "

Meredith looked out toward the pecan grove. The sky was brilliant and cloudless. The temperature was dropping. The wind ate right through her Florida coat. "He wanted me to come back here, and I didn't want to. I wanted to go somewhere else. Can't you understand that?"

Julia shook her head. "No. I can't. Make me understand."

"I was just so sick of him calling *me*, for years. He kept calling and trying to woo me back. Guilt me. So, that morning, I had been on the water all day. With my team. We were collecting samples. All up and down the river. I saw he'd called me thirty-five times. So, I called back, and told him I didn't care about him. I told him I never cared about him."

"But, why?"

"I wanted to hurt him."

Julia's eyes teared up. "I mean. He was sitting up here out of work, lonely as hell."

"I didn't know that. Julia, I'm not a bad person."

Julia shrugged, and shook her head. "Whatever you say."

Meredith got up to leave. "I need to go. I just want to go."

"So that's it? You come over here to tell me what I already know? That you broke my brother's heart."

"I'm leaving," Meredith said again to convince herself.

"You always acted like you were too good for us."

Meredith made it to the door. "I didn't mean to act like that. I don't believe I'm better than you. I really don't."

Julia nodded. Okay, she mouthed.

Meredith got her courage together. "You're right. That's not all. There's more."

Suddenly smug, Julia threw her feet up on a footstool.

"Tommy came to me. Last night. He was at the foot of my bed."

Julia was quiet. Meredith had never been able to read that woman. She was either hot or cold. Nothing in between. Meredith waited.

Julia's words came slowly. "That son of a bitch. That goddamn—"

Meredith's fists clinched. She felt perspiration over her lip like when she was inside.

Julia's face went red. "He came to you? To *you?*" she shouted. "After all I did for that boy. I fed him, clothed him, let him stay here for years. And, he came to *you?*"

Meredith wanted to say that it wasn't a pretty thing. It wasn't something she would prefer to have happened to anyone. "The thing is. He said he was the messenger. That he had a message from you to me."

"What? That I said for you to go to hell? Is that what he said? Because I already said that."

She laughed a kind of mean laugh that gave Meredith chills.

"Well? What did he tell you?"

What Tommy said revealed her own guilt. Isn't that what dreams did? They finagled with what was eating at you, and then they revealed it in the form of garish cartoons. "You know how dreams are," Meredith shrugged. "I woke up."

Julia frowned.

Meredith searched for something encouraging to say. She thought of Tommy's dimples, his sly grin. "He looked real good."

Julia perked up. "Was he happy?"

Meredith remembered Tommy's talon fingers, his angry face. Julia waited, desperate. "Yes," she said. "He was very happy."

"You think he'll come see you again? Because if he does—" Julia stopped, and clenched her fists.

Meredith half laughed, expecting Julia to say something along the lines of, "Because if he does, I will kick his ass," but instead the woman's eyes filled, and she could barely finish her sentence. "You tell him I want to talk to him." She put her face in her hands, and sobbed. "Okay? I need to."

Meredith put her hand on Julia's. "Oh, honey. I promise. I promise."

Julia nodded, then looked away. Meredith followed her gaze to the pecan orchard, gray and leafless after harvest. When they were like this, it seemed unlikely they would ever bloom again.

Meredith returned to the house for her purse. Hank slept on, despite the football game's blaring halftime show, a blur of flags and majorettes unfolding across the screen. Meredith picked up the remote control to mute the marching band, then set it down. Hank was a sleeper who thrived on noise. She arranged a Crimson Tide blanket over his wide shoulders.

Outside, an object caught Meredith's eye. Stooping, she reached for a forgotten pecan still packed in its outer casing. She peeled it away, slipped the smooth nut in her coat pocket, instinctively glancing to the porch stoop where old man Billups held court for years. He claimed to know when a single pecan was missing. The forgotten fruit was warm in her palm; she could almost taste the pulp, nutty and bitter, the aroma of ancient groves. She welcomed memories that came to her with the reverie of a half-time show: long-ago barrel fires on harvest nights, drinking till dawn, pitching beer cans into the flames. She thought of what Julia said, and wondered what *was* the likelihood of Tommy visiting again? Was there a possibility he might forgive her for not loving him? The giant trees closed in around her with their ghosts; she stepped away. There was a new windshield on the car, a long drive ahead.

Hurricane Machine

TO FRANCIS PELLICER, IT SEEMED BLASPHEMOUS to build
an artificial storm. Even at this rudimentary level with hot plates and
Masonite-paneled walls and aluminum pie plates, all Francis could
think about was the brine-burned pall the previous hurricanes had
cast over St. Augustine. But as he sat at the garage worktable, Francis
thought if he could give his brother, Emory, or, even himself, a
few moments of peace in this life, he'd try anything. At his side,
the World Book Encyclopedia 50th Anniversary Edition was open
to the diagram, and Francis memorized it as he secured a stovepipe
to an angle iron frame, removed drop handle knobs from the beat-
up chest of drawers he'd refinished for Miss Lonnie Triay. These
chipped porcelain knobs would make perfect handles for the sliding
panels; shifting the doors left and right controlled direction of the
coiling vapors, determined southern or northern hemisphere storms.

Francis headed across the backyard to the house to check on Emory
and find their grandmother's hot plate. It was late February, two weeks
past the traditional bloom of the azaleas. At the back door, Francis
stopped as he did four times a day to check the redbud and the dogwood,
the sentinels of spring, for a hint of baby bloom, but there was nothing.
This was his favorite time of year, when deep-shaded yards up and down
Masters Drive flushed with peppermint pink and cotton white azaleas,
some of these bushes decades old, left to grow as tall and wide as small
houses. But this year spring had already come to St. Augustine—in
November—and the question was: Can there be a second?

The 2004 hurricane season included three of the costliest storms in Florida history thus far, and two of the most menacing storms to hit St. Augustine in a hundred years. Meteorologists said the season would always be known for its record-breaking oddities. Alex, the first storm, didn't form until July 31, six weeks after the season began, and more than half of the 16 storms brushed the United States. The first to hit St. Augustine was Frances, the female version of the name—not Francis—though every time the storm was mentioned in front of Francis, people snickered as if he was a tempest himself. And, then there was Jeanne. Jeanne raged across Hispaniola as a Category 3, then reorganized into a Category 2, doubled backed in a perfect loop across the Atlantic, landing in Florida two miles from where Frances set down.

The winds from Frances and Jeanne were so violent they coughed salt spray up to ten miles inland burning the crown of sweet gums and sycamores, mulberry and fig trees, and faithful perennials—lip stick bushes, trumpet vines, night-blooming jasmine. On Masters Drive, Francis's front lawn was untouched, but the back yard facing the ocean was saturated with deep tissue trauma, its grass the texture of spent hay stalks. Salt chewed its way up trunks of palm trees, attacking ancient wisteria, nettling water oaks and red cedars. The streets flooded with ocean water, swelling up between sewer grate bars, pooling at the roots of magnolia trees.

On Thanksgiving Day the weather turned as sunny and humid as May. Mulberries fruited, wisteria and night-blooming jasmine bloomed. Foliage that had been forced into false winter by the salt burn simply misunderstood the cues. To them, winter was over.

This morning as Francis stood outside his kitchen door, at the base of the redbud, running his hand up and down the lower bare limbs, the words of Miss Lonnie came to him as she'd stood here last fall shaking her head at this very tree's purple blossoms: "In all my days," she'd said. "In all my living days. What will become of the true spring?"

EMORY WAS ON HIS BELLY WATCHING Match Game '76, his strawberry hair sticky with fettuccini alfredo. Sometimes he woke Francis in the middle of the night by planting a Klondike ice cream sandwich on his chest, then paced and hummed until Francis opened it for him. This morning at 5:45, Emory was hungry for a Stouffer's frozen dinner. When Francis microwaved it, Emory refused a napkin or utensils. Francis pleaded, "Bub, please be civilized," but Emory glared, ate with his hands, ran cream sauce through his hair. Later, he'd attempted to wash Emory's hair, but it was still matted. Now Emory was quiet and had on all his clothes and for that, Francis was grateful.

"Hey bubby. Ready to match the stars?" Francis asked.

"Match Game 76. Match Game 76," Emory answered Francis, his voice surging like the show's host, Gene Rayburn.

Francis remembered the game show from his own childhood, could recite a few of the Boxcar Bertha questions, but Emory memorized answers verbatim, down to the precise inflection of the celebrities' voices. He repeated some more than others, preferring a Betty White answer he'd heard a year ago. Francis couldn't even recall what the question had been.

Francis watched from the kitchen as Rayburn read the question, "Dumb Dora is so dumb." Rayburn said, then paused to allow the studio audience to chime in, "How dumb is she?"

"Dumb Dora is so dumb, " Rayburn began. "That she—"

Emory pulled his knees to his chest, rocked back and forth, then put his face to the warm screen of the television. "Polyester. I have to say poly. Poly-ester."

"Oh, Bubby, we missed the rest of the question, but I'll be damned if you don't sound just like Betty White."

"Poly-ester. Polyester," he said. "I would have to say."

In the kitchen, Francis dragged a stepladder to the cupboard. The house was built in the 1920s, the shelves deep and endless. He climbed up past Mason jars of pickled datil peppers, fig preserves, boxes of elbow macaroni. Their grandmother, Bebe, had been dead ten months, but Francis couldn't bring himself to eat the food.

Bebe kept everything. The hot plate was there, along with a Kenmore toaster in its original box. Francis had a perfectly fine toaster oven on the kitchen counter, so he'd check this one for repairs, sell it in his shop. The hot plate was the one Bebe used in her room to heat chicken soup and hot cocoa with marshmallows. Francis stood in the doorway watching Emory, estimated how much longer he had before Match Game was over. He scratched his nose, his fingers smelled of encyclopedia pages, mildewed and ancient. Rayburn stood in front of Charles Nelson Reilly, read the second round question. "Georgie Porgie said, 'I kiss the girls and make them cry, and Horrible Hanna says, oh that's nothing, I kiss the boys," Rayburn hesitated, winked at Brett Somers, and said, "And, make them blank.'

Emory answered, "Polyester. I would have to say. Because I like it. Polyester."

"Be right back, Bub," Francis said. "Working on something for you."

He left Richard Dawson and Fannie Flagg poking fun at Brett Somers, and Charles Nelson Reilly lighting his pipe, and went to the garage. The house fronted Masters Drive, but the garage behind the house faced Evergreen Street, a narrow limestone alley road that ran parallel to Masters Drive on the west and Ravenswood on the east. The garage served as Francis' small appliance shop, and a sign that read, "Pellicer Repairs," hung in neon orange letters on white plywood. He fixed vacuum cleaners, kitchen appliances, televisions. On Saturday mornings, Emory in tow, Francis made the yard sale rounds in search of items he could refurbish and resale. At his worktable, Francis secured the hot plate, tightened the screws on the angle iron frame.

Emory was twenty years old, a late developer, or in light of everything, Francis thought, a late bloomer. Everything about Emory was delayed, and he'd only just begun to feel the hormonal changes in his body. Francis frequently found the boy with his hands down his pants, jacking off in the middle of the kitchen or the living room, and once completely undressed, Emory masturbated in the garage just footsteps away as Francis talked to a customer in his shop about the blown-out bulbs in his television set. But the storms that came through this past fall had stopped Emory in his tracks. He'd been mesmerized by the sheeting rain, bent trees, far-flung plastic lawn chairs.

After all the research people did on boys like Emory, it was funny that Francis, repairman of Oysterizer blenders and Whirlpool air purifiers, was the one to figure out how to fix his brother. This wasn't *fixing* Emory in the sense of making him like Francis. The professionals had tried that. There'd been words thrown around—Autism, Asperger's, Hydrocephalus, Microcephaly—none of which completely fit Emory's unique behaviors. Francis always assumed this was why his mother left. She couldn't stand it anymore. In the beginning, they'd had him crawl through a maze of cardboard boxes, something about forcing alignment of the actions of his body to make the brain heal. Emory, a toddler then, had screamed, refused to go into the box. Later, a woman came to the house with smudge sticks of white sage, burned incense in the coquina flower pots out front. Bebe said that was when she knew Grace, his mother, had lost her mind.

"But I was normal," Francis told Bebe. "Why'd she leave me?"

"Honey," she'd said, angry tears in her eyes. "When Evelyn Grace Pellicer left here, she left us all."

FRANCIS TOOK EMORY BY THE HAND, led him down the lane past the Tom Thumb convenience store and the back yards of his neighbors—the Manucys, the Paseos, the Fornales, Miss Lonnie's.

Until three and a half weeks weeks ago, Emory attended Tender Loving Care, a state-funded day care for mentally disabled adults. Emory caught the white van each morning at eight and went out to an enormous facility on Dobbs Road where he was with others like him. They sang nursery rhymes, learned life skills, danced and went for walks. He was there until 3:30 five days a week, and Francis was able to get his chores done, keep up with his repair business, spend evenings and weekends with Emory. But the week of Emory's twentieth birthday, the State of Florida temporarily cut off all funds for the mentally disabled. The director of the St. Augustine TLC, Delia Oxendine, assured Francis she'd get the funding from Governor Jeb Bush if it was the last thing she did. But that was three weeks ago, and Francis had been calling her office every day. He'd left a dozen messages.

Inside Hamblin's, Francis said to Emory, "You can watch the key maker while I'm getting what I need."

Emory liked the way the table vibrated as the grinding machine carved silver and gold blanks. For the past month, every time he took Emory to the store, he dropped off house, car and shop keys at the counter. Francis wondered if it had the same affect the hurricane force winds had on Emory. Whatever it was, the key carving station bought Francis a few moments of time to walk around the store and pick up the items he needed. Otherwise, Emory held every object to see how it felt when he hummed against it. One visit could take two hours. Since he'd discovered this quick remedy, Francis had eight sets of every single key he owned.

Francis took out one of these eight sets and his wallet. He'd been making do since Bebe died. Special compensation brought Francis his brother's social security so he did his best to piece it all together. They had enough to pay the bills, and there would always be figs and datil peppers. Francis waved at Dean the key man.

"Be right there," Dean said.

"Stay here, Bub," Francis said. "Watch the keys, and wait for me here."

There were two kinds of pie plates, a deep dish, and a shallow. Francis picked up a three-pack of deep, and heading toward the dairy section, spotted a rack of party decorations. Cellophane rolls, balloons, crepe paper. He held a roll of rose-tinted cellophane, imagined how it would crackle like sheets of rain. He'd scissor long thin ribbons, tape them from the ceiling of Emory's second floor room. The wild helix from the hurricane machine would rattle the streamers, and maybe they'd reflect the light like water beading on glass. He took a second, a bright roll of topaz.

In the dairy section, Francis was staring down at the cheese, deciding between sharp and mild, when he heard Margie Hamblin's crisp voice over the microphone. "Francis Pellicer. Come to produce. Francis Pellicer." There was urgency in her voice that made Francis run, the milk jug hanging by his thumb, pie plates quivering like distant thunder.

EMORY HAD NOT BOTHERED TO UNFASTEN his khakis. Francis had searched JC Penney for pants difficult to quickly unzip, but Emory had found a way to reach far into them, and there he was, leaning against a display of plum tomatoes. Mrs. Hamblin shooed customers away, and she ran too, covering her face. Dean the key man attempted to stop him, but the pyramid of tomatoes collapsed, sent tomatoes tumbling.

"Stop, bub. Stop," Francis said. He slapped Emory's arm, tomatoes underfoot, all the while the boy's eyes fixated upwards. Francis threw his jacket around Emory, let him finish his business. Some nights when Francis was alone with his brother, it did not surprise him that their mother had finally run off with Frankie Whetstone, become a crack dealer on Jacksonville's Westside. Police found her face down in the median of Casset Avenue when Francis was twelve, Emory seven. For weeks, Emory stood at the front window, waiting. "Look at the window, look at the window," he'd say, waiting for her to drive up in front of the house. To this day, Emory called out for her at night, "Look at the window. Look at the window." Francis told him that she was asleep like an angel in heaven. But that wasn't something Emory could understand. "Look at the window, look at the window," he'd say. Francis found him downstairs at night, pacing and repeating. "Look at the window." Emory grunted, and Francis held the coat higher. His mother had been gone so long, Francis could hardly remember her voice, but at times like this one of her wry sayings would come to him, and right there in Hamblin's store, he heard her voice plain as day. "Baby, put the piggy back in the poke."

When Emory was finished, Francis took his hand, wiped it on his own jacket. Mrs. Hamblin, holding back the tears, met him at the door. It was then he'd realized they'd smashed tomatoes with their boots, tracked pulpy prints across the store. He held up the cellophane, the milk, the pie plates. "I didn't pay yet."

"All my customers have run off," she said, shooing his groceries. "One lady had a full cart. She just walked out."

Mrs. Hamblin took Francis by the arm, her fingers a stern trap on his elbow. Emory watched his reflection in the mirrored door, closing and opening his fists. Francis tried to explain. She gripped him harder. "Don't bring him back in here again."

Francis looked into her damp green eyes. This woman had known his mother, gone to Ketterlinus High School with his grandmother.

"I promise," Francis said, feeling the pinch of Mrs. Hamblin's hold soften. "I won't ever bring him back."

FRANCIS TOOK A COLD COORS TO THE back yard, sat down
in the Adirondack, stared into the wide bed of sword ferns that had
long ago taken over the yard, their perforated blades speckled with
falling light. Emory was inside spinning in circles, watching or mostly
listening to Jeopardy. Jeopardy had been Bebe's favorite, and once
Francis and Bebe were eating dinner in the kitchen watching it on the
little countertop TV set. Emory walked in and just as you please answered
Alex Trebek's question, "Part that makes a lightbulb light up."

"Filament," Emory had said.

Bebe had grabbed Francis' hand. She mouthed, "Damn."

They sat in silence, waited for the next question, a $200 one.

"You do this to Crepe Suzettes by lighting brandy, rum, or cognac."

"Flame," said Emory. "Flame. Flame."

They'd sat there while he answered them all, until he'd become
distracted by his hands, and walked back to the living room, humming
into them, feeling his mouth buzz against his palm.

Bebe said she'd call the paper, have them do a write-up. He's
a savant, she'd said. A genius. The next night Francis walked into
the other room, just before the show and saw that Jeopardy was on
another network an hour before. Still, Bebe had reasoned, the boy
had a better memory than most folks who people insist are normal.
Francis took a sip of his beer, stared out at the triangle tips of the
darkening ferns. He wished people like Mrs. Hamblin realized this
about Emory, how it was difficult to manage such a mind.

Francis glanced down at his clean boots. With the garden hose,
he'd washed tomato from their shoes, then put Emory, howling, into
the shower. He would call Delia Oxendine again tomorrow. Thinking
about the coming weeks or months on his own with Emory—the
hours it would take to do even the simplest of errands—exhausted
him. How was he to work in his shop? If he kept Emory with him,
he was constantly interrupted, and if he left him inside in front of
the TV, he needed to leave his work to check on him. Francis was
about to go inside and cook white rice with butter, fry up a couple of
crappies he had in the freezer when all of a sudden out the back of
the Tom Thumb came August Usina. She lobbed a trash bag up and
into the dumpster. Hands on her hips, she turned and saw Francis.

Francis swallowed hard, cleared his throat. Dear God, he thought. Is that really her? She stared at him, paused, then walked up the lane. Despite the chill in the air, she wore cutoff jeans, a T-shirt under a red and yellow Tom Thumb vest.

"How long you been back?" was all he could muster. The first thing that came to him was I told you so, but he didn't need to say it as her shrug said it all.

"About three weeks."

Francis nodded. He couldn't believe he hadn't seen her or heard she was in town. "How long you been working at the Tom?"

"Five days, but who's counting?"

He noticed her eyeing his beer. "Thirsty?" he said.

"Didn't think you'd ever ask." She came close, took one long drag on the can, then downed the rest of it.

Francis could smell the cigarettes, the sweat, the Dove soap. It hurt to look at her.

"I'm sorry," she said, crumpling the can with her fist. "I didn't deserve that." She dropped the can on the ground. "Neither did you."

"It's nothing," he said.

August studied the road toward the store. She'd propped the back door with a brick. "I can hardly stand that place." She dipped her thumbs in her back pockets. "So. You been all right?"

"Me?" Francis said. "Guess so."

"How's bubby?"

"He's good. Growing up."

She smiled, looked toward the house. "I bet." she said, pointing the toe of her sneaker in the sand.

Francis couldn't think of anything else to say. Finally August turned and headed back up the lane.

"See you?" Francis called after her.

She stopped in the middle of the lane, thinking. "You forgive me?" she finally said.

It caught Francis off guard. Forgive her? He'd put her out of his mind, hoped he'd never lay eyes on her again. But forgive her? Never. But face to face, he couldn't admit it. "I let you drink my beer, didn't I?"

She stared as if she wasn't satisfied with the answer, and just when Francis thought she might smile, or come back, she jogged off to the store.

THAT NIGHT, FRANCIS SET THE HURRICANE machine on an old coffee table in Emory's room. It stood three-feet high, two feet wide. He filled the aluminum pie pan, heated up the hotplate. The boiling water created warm spools of mist. Francis slid the panels to the left—forcing the vapors to spiral counterclockwise into a northern hemisphere storm. Soon, the air shot up through the stovepipe. Suddenly a breeze blew the cellophane sashes.

"It worked!" Francis said. "Bubby!"

He found his brother in the middle of the stairs, his boxers at his knees. "Oh, come on, Bub." Emory slapped him off, kept pulling on himself, but Francis shoved him to the room. "You got to see this."

At the sight of the man-made gusts, the rippling streamers, Emory stopped in the middle of the room. He soon began to hum, and sing, calm as he'd been on the nights Jeanne and Francis ploughed through St. Augustine. He stood still, allowing Francis to situate his pants, then sat on the floor cooing and rocking back and forth. Francis filled a second pan when that one boiled off, and then a third.

"Don't touch," he told Emory. "Hot. Understand?"

"Polyester," Emory answered. "Starring Adam West as himself. Polyester."

Francis looked out the bedroom window down into the yard below at the brick patio, the lopsided coquina urns spilling over with black peat, the fern beds, the Adirondack poised toward the limestone lane and August Usina. August. He'd always wondered about her name. Had she been born in August, conceived in August? Were her parents married in August? Was she named for St. Augustine? To this day, he didn't know and couldn't believe he still wanted to.

AUGUST DIDN'T COME BACK THE NEXT NIGHT or the next. But some evenings she left her post at the Tom Thumb cash register and leaned on the great white oak tree in Miss Lonnie's backyard, smoked a cigarette. From his chair, Francis watched her in the dark, wondered if she thought of him, if she regretted the hurt she'd caused. Some nights, a Ford diesel idled out back of the store. Francis didn't have to listen too long to recognize Randall Manucy's gravelly voice. They pitched their empty beer cans in the truck bed. Sometimes they fought.

"Don't you tell me what to do," August said one night with such sass it made Francis smile. The back door to the Tom Thumb slammed; Randall sped off, honking his way up Masters Drive.

There in the dark, Francis said her name aloud. "August." He closed his eyes, saw rough oyster shelled walls, coquina concrete blocks of the Castillo de San Marcos, the inlet past Rattlesnake Island, mile marker 62. He saw her short shorts, denim frayed and wispy, the small gray tattoo of a dolphin on her left ankle just above the curve of her Achilles. He'd forgotten lots of things, simply shoved them away. Why sit and let memories fester? August Usina would never be his. She wasn't capable of loving a man. What was it his grandmother had said? She was a tease, a hurtful one at that. But as he began to think about Emory and TLC and Pellicer's Repairs, his mind wandered to the way August's T-shirts fit, how her ribs felt beneath his palms, the soft underside of her thighs, and suddenly he'd gone hard.

THE NEXT DAY HE WORKED MOST OF the morning on Miss Lonnie's chest of drawers. He sanded it, painted two coats of a pale blue, Nurture by Sherwin Williams, that got prettier and more like an April sky as it dried. The brand new crystal knobs were miniature clouds.

"My word," Miss Lonnie said. "This is the most beautiful thing I've ever seen."

It made Francis proud, and he stood back enjoying it with her.

"You ought to do more furniture," she said.

"Believe I just might."

"Honey," she said, sitting down to write him a check. Francis admired her perfect cursive handwriting. "I heard about what happened at the hardware store."

Francis shut his eyes. Surely the entire town had heard by now. What if his customers were disgusted, afraid to come by?

"I can watch Emory if you need me."

Francis thought of the tomatoes, Mrs. Hamblin's message to him over the intercom. What if Emory actually did something, like rub up against Miss Lonnie? He couldn't live with himself if that happened. "No. No. He's hard to control. You just don't know."

She nodded, patted his hand. "You want me to talk to Margie Hamblin? It's not fair to forbid you in her store."

"She's in the right. She was awfully upset."

"You ought to call the governor's office yourself. At least try to get them to find you a program."

Francis looked over at Emory, his hands filthy with melted M&M's. "What if they say no? What if they don't want him anywhere?"

"Francis," Miss Lonnie had him by the hand, the same way his grandmother used to do, whether she was talking about how good a job he'd done mowing the lawn or whether it was to talk sense into him when he was doubting himself. "You can't raise him on your own."

The way Miss Lonnie said this scared Francis, as if she knew how his life would turn out. Through the garage window, Francis saw the crumbling coquina urns, overturned cement planters, the rogue sword ferns that had robbed almost all of the growing space in the backyard. It was only a matter of time before they filled in the front lawn. He picked up his truck keys, took Emory by the hand. "Let's get this chest of drawers loaded, see how it looks at your house."

THAT AFTERNOON, WHILE EMORY watched Match Game, Francis called Delia Oxendine.

"I've been in Tallahassee," she said. "That place is no St. Augustine. Let me tell you that right now."

Francis cleared his throat. "What did they say?"

"Program's pulled for good. They want me to place all my clients in the workplace. Walmart. Target—"

"But Emory can't work."

"I know. I know. There's only about four that can. I sat right there in front of Jeb himself and told him I got people wearing diapers. Some are head bangers with helmets. How am I supposed to find these folks work?" Delia said. Her chair squeaked, and she sighed. "I'm not going to give up. But who knows how long this will take."

Francis stared into the living room where Emory spun in circles, hummed the tune to Jeopardy. Years, Francis thought. It could take years.

"Poly-ester," Emory said.

"Patty told me you called last week. Sounds like you've been having a rough time with Emory."

Francis hesitated. He didn't like to talk about it. "It seems to happen anytime. Anywhere. You wouldn't believe the scene at the grocery store. I can't control him."

"Well, the thing is, you *can't* control it."

"It's not like I'm giving him Playboys and Hustlers or something and saying have at it."

Delia laughed. "I know you aren't, honey. It's physiological. You can't stop him. It's not like Emory knows it's even wrong to do that in public. I had a client one time who used to get aroused by the washing machine when it was on rinse cycle."

"But a key machine? A stack of plum tomatoes?"

"Listen, I have a list of some good sitters."

"Medicaid won't pay."

"But if you just need them once or twice a week, it shouldn't be too hard on your budget." She paused. Her chair squeaked again. "Francis?"

"Yes?"

"They've seen it all."

Francis thought of that full cart of groceries left behind, the ruined plum tomatoes. He should have offered to help Mrs. Hamblin clean up, pay her for the trouble. As Delia rattled off the phone numbers, Francis didn't even pick up a pencil.

"You got that, honey?"

"Yes ma'am. I appreciate it."

EMORY REQUESTED THE HURRICANE machine by shaking the cellophane. He came to Francis in the middle of the night with fistfuls of artificial rain, and Francis would restring them, remind Emory not to pull them down. The aluminum pie plate held two cups of water and evaporated quickly. The night after he spoke to Delia Oxendine and declined her list of sitters for Emory, Francis added ten-inch steel platform legs so the generator stood taller, allowing for a two-quart saucepan to sit beneath it. He wasn't certain of the boil-off rate, so he'd keep an eye on the clock. Maybe one day he could turn on the storm for Emory then run down to Hamblin's for basic groceries. He could always ask Miss Lonnie to pick him up some things, but he never intended to become indebted to anyone. Emory was his responsibility; he'd have to work this out.

Francis filled the pan, and when the vapors kinked upward, Francis opened the panels to the right. As a southern hemisphere storm developed in Emory's bedroom, Francis sat and watched his brother. He'd truly never seen him so peaceful. The streamers danced against the window. Emory hummed to the tick tick of the intoxicating rain, the spinning air, and Francis left him, took a flashlight outside to examine the redbud tree. He was beginning to believe that somehow between stubborn hope and the hurricane machine he might make this life doable. As he climbed the stepladder, searching bare branches, he heard his name.

"Francie?" It was August, her voice slurred. She held a six-pack of Miller Lite over her head. She wore a white T-shirt beneath her Tom Thumb vest, no cutoffs this time, but full-length jeans.

Francis looked toward the house. "I can't."

"Just one?"

"I got things to do," he said. A tease, he reminded himself. She doesn't know what love is. "Won't Randall be coming for you soon?"

She ignored his question. "Come on, I owe you one. Or, four." She sat on the Adirondack, yanked two beers from their loops.

Francis left the flashlight on the lower rung of the stepladder, pulled a worn lawn chair around to face August, reluctantly popped open the can. He'd have one beer, that was all. Francis stared down at the dolphin's fin, then at August's knees as she nudged them against his.

"I'm not long for this world. Not long at all," she said, sipping her beer. "Remember the last time we kissed?"

Francis looked into his beer. They were sitting right about here. How could he forget? And, she'd been crying. Sobbing so he'd gone inside for tissues. Randall was cheating on her. Again. She'd had enough, insisted she was leaving him for good. This time she'd go to her ex-husband's in Macon, Georgia, she'd said. He was the only man who'd ever truly loved her. Francis had tried to make her stay. And, she had. Two glorious nights, and then one morning she was gone. Just like that.

"No," Francis said. "I don't recall it."

August got out of her chair and knelt beside Francis. She held his face in her hands. "And you're a liar." She kissed his chin, his mouth. She tasted of cigarettes, sour lemon drops.

Francis pushed her away. "Stop," he said.

"Why? Are you mad at me?"

Francis stood. "No note, no phone call. No explanation. And, here you are back in town. You went straight back to Randall, not me."

She leaned in to him, looked up with her brown eyes. "You don't know how bad I feel about that. I wish I could explain it."

She kissed him again, ran her hands inside his shirt. "Please," she said.

"We can't," Francis said.

"Give me one good reason."

Francis stared into her face. She'd never understand. Or, would she? He wondered how it would feel to hurt her back. He pulled August onto his lap, kissed her neck, inhaled the Dove. Briefly, he thought of Emory in his stormy room, the generator's hum, the trembling rain. Francis unsnapped August's bra, and she slipped up her shirt so he could kiss her breasts. Just this one time, he told himself, and then he'd never speak to her again—he'd show her how it felt. He pulled her to his chest.

Something gold and sparkling made him look toward the house. Emory was there, face pressed to the windowpane, flames above his head.

"Emory!" Francis said. He took the steps two at a time. There was the smell of burning plastic, and smoke filled the room. Emory was half-naked, huddled beside the bed, his sweat pants on the floor. August hesitated in the doorway, taking in the generator, the empty boiler pan flung to the floor, the red coils of the hot plate, Emory's boxers.

"What—" she started.

At the sight of August, Emory yelled, "Look at the window." The rose and topaz streamers were ash snakes. A green curtain panel had caught fire, too, and Francis ran to the bathroom, grabbed a damp towel, flapped at the smoking fabric, then pulled it to the floor and stomped it.

"Look at the window," Emory said. "Look at the window."

"Bubby, your mama's gone—" August started in a voice so tender it made Francis' knees weak. She'd remembered. She'd only been here two days, but she remembered. "Tell him, Francie."

"Stop it," Francis told her. "He means he *saw* us. Don't you get it? He was *watching* us."

Emory kicked Francis, cried louder. "Look at the window," he said, pointing at August.

"He saw us," Francis said, this time to himself. He felt sick to his stomach at the thought of Emory seeing him kissing August, becoming aroused by that. He quietly took Emory's hand. Pink blisters pocked his palm. "Oh, Bub, I told you not to touch." Francis wrapped the bedspread around Emory's waist, sat on the bed, rocked him back and forth.

Outside, the truck pulled up in the lane, its reckless muffler brewing. There was a quick honk, then another one, longer, louder.

"Go on," Francis said, not looking up at August.

"I don't want to."

"Go," Francis said.

"But—"

Francis couldn't imagine her truly ever staying here, or anywhere. As he spoke, he remembered the finality in Mrs. Hamblin's voice. "Go and don't come back."

Finally, she went downstairs, and Francis watched her from the window. She paused at the Adirondack, reached behind her back, re-hooked her bra. Please, Francis thought. Don't go. Look at the window. August seemed to consider the silent request until Randall honked the horn again. She grabbed the remaining four beers, ran across the yard, Miller Lite swinging from plastic hooks. Up the lane, the truck door slammed, the engine revved, chased up Masters Drive. Why had he ever thought there'd be anything more?

"Look at the window," Emory said.

"Tell me what happened, Bubby," he said, quietly. "Tell me."

Emory sniffled, squeezed his eyes. More than anything Francis wished for a real conversation with Emory, not clever quips from Match Game. He rubbed his brother's back, tried to piece together what happened. Maybe he'd gone to play with the streamers, had seen Francis with his hands up August's shirt. Maybe in excitement, Emory knocked off the boiling water, pulled the rain down onto the burner of the hot plate. Or, maybe, he'd been locked inside himself, calling to the window to bring their mother home.

"I'm so sorry," Francis said. "So sorry."

When Emory was asleep, Francis took the generator downstairs, set it on the kitchen table. He'd take it apart tomorrow, see what he could reuse. Or, maybe he'd throw the entire goddamn contraption in the trash. He thought of a line from the encyclopedia: A real hurricane begins when the sun heats the ocean producing a rising cloud of warm moist air. Real, Francis thought. Weather can't be invented; Mother Nature does what she desires.

At sunrise, Francis went downstairs, faced the backyard and the limestone lane as if she would reappear, if everything would reappear—the cold six-pack, her cutoffs, the red and yellow Tom Thumb vest. The flashlight and the stepladder were still beside the redbud, and only then did he remember what he'd intended to do last night. Carefully, Francis climbed to the top step, inspected the lean limbs. There on the end of the second highest branch, was one ripe bead on the verge of furious lavender.

Acknowledgments

This book had a tremendous support system. It would have been impossible without:

Kimberly Verhines and Meredith Janning at Stephen F. Austin University Press. I am forever grateful.

The best book club: Charlyn, Jody, Maureen, Jean, Sherry, Diane, Sue, Karen, Sandy, Ann, and Becky, and forever missed, Sally and Diana.

My Alabama family for all the stories and love; my Lake Annie family, especially John and Kathy McGuire, for the Clint tales and inspiration, and the kids for their crazy shenanigans.

My earliest workshop readers turned lifelong pals. Tons of thanks for the valuable feedback on these stories: Jim Herod, Annell Gordon, Sandi Hutcheson, Karen Kravit, Scott Archer Jones, Joy Dickinson, Frances Neville, Stephanie Josey, and Helena Rho; David Beaty of the FIU Seaside days for sharing my deep affection for the short story; and Cindy Chinelly, from all the workshops and beyond, for your friendship.

Decades of encouragement and sound advice from Ron and Mary Ann Barzso, Liz Robbins, Deny Howeth, Zack Strait, Jill Coupe, Linda Newton, and Randy Glazer.

The roundtable: Jay Szczepanski, Stephen Kampa, and Judith Burdan, for the much-needed laughter and moral support.

Life-changing weekly workshops at a picnic table under the palm trees. Here's to EOF with all my love: Jean Dowdy, Maureen Welch, Six-Word Sherry Dickerson, and Dasher.

The wisdom, friendship, and guidance of John Dufresne, my workshop buddy and best writing teacher on the planet; steadfast friend and fellow plotter, Laura Lee Smith—thanks for always having the answers; Marcie Alvarado Molloy, generous listener and loyal friend, for making me laugh for 35 years.

My family for their unyielding support: My mom, Sandra Bradley, for always being there, and always reading everything; the best brother ever, Kenneth, for his friendship and humor; Katy, Maxwell, Riley and Evie for being the absolute coolest. And, my deepest gratitude to Craig, Isaac and Phoebe for their unwavering love; I'm so very lucky.

The following stories have appeared previously in these journals:

"King of the Mountain," *Southern Humanities Review*

"Cheating Time," *The Louisville Review*

"Like She Stole it," *Needle: A Magazine of Noir*

"Spillway," *Bayou*

"How to Draw a Circle," *Kalliope*

"Hurricane Machine," *Natural Bridge*

"Grounded" *The Broadkill Review*

Photo Credit: Phoebe Barzso

KIM BRADLEY grew up in Monroeville, Alabama, and studied journalism at Auburn University. She received an MFA in creative writing from the University of New Orleans. Her work has appeared in *Southern Humanities Review, Natural Bridge, Bayou, Southern Indiana Review, The Louisville Review, Real South Magazine, Needle: A Magazine of Noir, The Broadkill Review,* and *Saw Palm: Florida Literature and Art.* She teaches creative writing and first-year writing at Flagler College in St. Augustine, Florida, where she is an assistant professor of English.

CPSIA information can be obtained
at www.ICGtesting.com
Printed in the USA
LVHW050540190322
713645LV00004B/15

9 781622 882359